CHRISTMAS OF THE DEAD

CANTHONY GIANGREGORIO

Christmas of the Dead

Anthony Giangregorio

OTHER BOOKS BY ANTHONY GIANGREGORIO

THE DEAD WATER SERIES
DEADWATER
DEADWATER: Expanded Edition
DEADRAIN
DEADCITY
DEADWAVE
DEAD HARVEST
DEAD UNION
DEAD VALLEY
DEAD GRAVE
DEADTOWN/HOMEWARD BOUND
DEAD SALVATION
DEAD ARMY

ALSO BY THE AUTHOR
SOUL EATER
THE DARK
DARK PLACES
BOTTOM OF THE NINTH
RISE OF THE DEAD
KINGDOM OF THE DEAD
THE MONSTER UNDER THE BED
DEAD END: A ZOMBIE NOVEL
DEAD TALES: SHORT STORIES TO DIE FOR
DEAD MOURNING: A ZOMBIE HORROR STORY
WARRIORS OF THE APOCALYPSE 1&2
ROAD KILL: A ZOMBIE TALE
COMEDY OF THE DEAD
CLAN OF THE BIGFOOT
DEAD OFFERINGS
DEADFREEZE
DEADFALL
DEADRAGE
BLOODRAGE

Table of Contents

DEAD CHRISTMAS

T'was the night before Dead Christmas, and all through the land,
Not a living creature was stirring, except a few severed hands.
The last family left alive, was barricaded inside,
While visions of death and carnage, danced in their minds.
The undead were hungry, as they searched for food,
And the humans knew their time was short, all of them in dire moods.

But then in the backyard, of this particular house,
There came a loud noise, and it wasn't a mouse.
Away to the back door, the family ran with haste,
For the dead were breaking in, there was no time to waste.

Moonlight bathed the new fallen snow,
As the family searched both high and then low.
But then did their searching eyes finally find,
It was a dead man in a Santa suit, and behind him more of his kind.

Though hard to believe, he was not false but the real deal,
And as he stumbled from his sleigh, eight undead reindeer snorted with zeal.
His eyes were glazed, his flesh pale and white,
And as he let out a low moan, anyone within earshot was chilled with fright.

Zombie Santa waved the undead horde onward,
And hundreds of animated corpses began to stumble forward.
As the ghouls began to break into the home,
The family cried out, their screams swallowed by undead moans.

The living dead began to feed, and the carnage was great,
As Zombie Santa looked on, the last human family suffering a terrible fate.
When all were killed and only bloody shards were left,
Santa climbed back into his sleigh, carrying a single severed head with some heft.

He held it aloft for all the zombies to see,
And reached inside to pull out the brains, and handed them to two ghouls, not three.

"The last humans are dead and we rule the land!
We are the true creatures God wants on hand.
Humans were weak, and we are strong,
And this night, our reach is long!"

"The dead walk the Earth, and so the world will burn,
Humans are gone, never to return.
So the next time you hug your loved ones, don't take them for granted,
Remember, how fast they can be supplanted."

CHRISTMAS IS DEAD

T'was the night before Christmas, when all through the morgue,
Not a creature was stirring, not even a corpse.
Its internal organs, were hung on a scale with care,
In hopes the mortician, would find cause of death.

The rest of the bodies, were snug in their deathbeds,
While visions of Heaven and Hell, danced in their heads.
The cadavers were wrapped, nice and tight in their body bags,
As the mortician settled down, with the day's bloody rags.

When out back in the cemetery, there came a loud sound.
The mortician investigated, as there was no one around.
Away to the back door, he flew like a wraith,
And tore open the portal, there was no time to waste.

The moon reigned down, over the new-fallen snow,
As the mortician searched, both high and then low.
When what to his searching eyes did he find,
But a corpse in a Santa suit was walking, the first of its kind.

The ghoul was stumbling, not too fast or too quick,
He knew in a flash, it was a living dead man named St. Nick.
His face was pale, his cheeks far from red,

And when he exhaled, it was foul, the legend surely dead.

Zombie Santa turned, and waved his claw-like hand,
And eight zombie reindeer, stumbled across the land.
"Kill them, Dasher Dancer, Prancer and Vixen!
 Eat their brains, Comet, Cupid, Donner and Blitzen!"

He shambled to his sleigh, and moaned to his deer,
Who joined him then, and snarled with a leer.
As zombie Santa and deer, flew off into the night,
The apocalypse had begun, the world over by first light.

The mortician heard Santa, call out to the night,
"Christmas is dead! It's no use to fight!
For the dead will walk, and eat your brains,
The world has ended, with blood and with pain."

So hug your kids, your pets and your mice,
Because the dead now live, their teeth like a vice.
And run for the hills, for your death is in sight
Christmas is dead, you can't stop the night.

The following story is about Santa Claus and a small boy named Timmy. Though there are no zombies in it, I hope you like it.

THE REAL SANTA CLAUS

Timmy had awoken to something but he didn't know what it was. Then he heard it again.

Snorting, and bells…like jingle bells?

He glanced to his clock on his nightstand and saw it was two hours past midnight.

It was Christmas!

Finally!

There was more noise and then there was the sound of something landing heavily in the living room. Muffled curses soon followed.

"Dad?" Timmy said softly. Maybe his father was putting out the presents for the next morning. He couldn't wait; he'd asked for the new Xbox and also a BB gun. He didn't think he was going to get the BB gun but hey, he'd asked anyway when sitting on Santa's lap at the mall.

More muttered curses and a loud *thunk* came to him and he slid out of bed, curious to see what was making so much racket. He made sure to take his stuffed bear Willie with him of course; just in case he needed protection. Willie might be stuffed, but he had courage and was strong and protected Timmy every night from the monsters under his bed.

As he tip-toed into the hallway and made his way past his parents' bedroom, he peeked inside. His dad was snoring like he was a lumberjack and the shape of his mom was right next to him.

That was weird. If his parents were both still sleeping, then who was making so much noise?

No, it couldn't be, but then again…

Timmy pulled his head away from the bedroom door and began running down the hallway, and realizing he was going too fast, he tried to put on the brakes. He began skating across the hardwood floor, his socks allowing him to 'ice skate.' He slid right into the back of the couch and fell onto his butt.

"Huh? What the hell was that?" a voice said and Timmy rolled over and quickly pushed up tight against the back of the couch. A shadow loomed over him a second later, as someone inspected the area behind the couch, which was lost in the shadows, and Timmy was well hidden.

"Huh, must be gettin' jumpy in my old age."

The shadow retreated and Timmy let out a soft sigh…he was safe.

More noise came to him and he heard the Christmas tree ornaments rattling as the man put items under it. The moon was high this night and the pale glow filtered into the room, casting everything in a yellow pallor.

Timmy, his heart in his throat, slowly raised his head over the back of the couch, so he could see who was in his house, and at the same time—with both hope and wonder—praying what he thought was happening was coming true.

If someone had been watching the couch, they would have seen Timmy's face slowly appear, like he was on a rising platform. His hair was first, followed by his forehead, then his eyes popped up from the top of the couch. Timmy's eyes went wide when he saw before him, standing in front of the Christmas tree, a man in a red suit with white trim.

(Author's note: *Yeah, I think we all know who this is so I'm not gonna go into all that 'bowl full of jelly junk' or his 'round belly' or his 'white beard' ect. I think you get it.*)

So anyway, back to Timmy.

Timmy's eyes were wide as he stared at Santa. He watched with wonder as the man worked, placing presents under the tree.

But the more Timmy watched Santa work, the more something seemed off about him.

For one thing, he smelled like cheap liquor. (Timmy knew this from when his dad went on business meetings and came home late. He would tuck Timmy in and his breath always smelled the same).

Another thing was Santa kept swearing as he worked. Timmy wasn't allowed to say those words but he knew them well from hearing his father use them. Not all the time but when something bad happened, like his dad was hammering in a nail and he missed and hit his thumb instead. Or Timmy had left one of his toys lying around on the floor in the living room or hallway and his dad accidentally stepped on it, or there was the time Timmy had left his bicycle in the driveway and his father had backed into it, scratching the bumper of the family car.

So yeah, Timmy knew those swear words well.

Santa went over to the milk and cookies on the table and picked up the glass of milk and took a big bite of one of the cookies. He winced as he sipped the milk—as if he didn't like the taste—and after dropping the cookie back to the plate, he reached inside his suit and pulled out a silver flask. Popping the top with his teeth, he poured something that Timmy didn't know was Vodka into the milk. After putting the flask away, Santa took another sip of milk and this time smiled...widely.

He went and sat down in Timmy's dad's easy chair and pulled out a pack of Lucky's, then lit one. Timmy saw the Zippo Santa used and noticed the initials KK on it.

(Authors note: *Kris Kringle, and if you don't know what I'm talking about, shame on you. Go watch Rankin and Bass' 'Santa Claus is Coming to Town,' then get back here, but I'm not waiting for you*).

Santa finished his milk and put the glass down, only he was a little tipsy now and the glass slid off the table. It smashed on the floor and Santa chuckled, not really caring. His cell phone rang and he pulled it out, opening it. "Go for big S."

He listened for a moment and said, "Look, Martha, we've been over this before. Now shut up and leave me alone. I'll be home when I'm home. And you can get your own damn cigarettes." He snapped the phone closed and let out a burp, then scratched his backside.

He shook his head to clear it and muttered something about "Damn elves not worth the food I feed them and it's a good thing they work for free," then went to the chimney opening. Getting down on his knees, and with a few more choice curses, he peered up into the shaft and yelled, "Are you idiots gonna toss down the rest of those presents or am I gonna have to bust some heads!"

Timmy couldn't believe what he was seeing and hearing, and he had to rub his eyes as if he was wiping away a mirage.

It was Santa, the *real* Santa, and though it was hard to believe, Timmy was discovering that yes, Santa Claus did exist.

And he was kind of a jerk.

YES, VIRGINIA, THERE IS A ZOMBIE SANTA CLAUS

It was well past midnight on Christmas Eve, and was now officially Christmas day.

A bright red sleigh filled with presents floated across the sky, a jolly man in a red suit its sole passenger.

Chris Kringle, or Santa Claus, to the world, leaned back in his seat as the reindeer cut through the clouds, their small bells jingling on their collars.

It had been a busy night so far but the southern hemisphere was finally finished.

Below, Haiti waited for its share of Christmas joy.

Pulling on the reins, he angled the sled downward, the drop enough to make his stomach jump. He laughed, long and loud. Even after all these years, he still didn't like to fly.

Moments later he was on his first roof top, a shanty-like home with a patched roof. He was in the poor part of town, but to him it all looked the same.

Rich or poor, he had a present for every child across the world.

Turning around, he reached into his magic sack; the voluminous red bag looking like it only had a few toys in it. But when he took a toy out of the bag, another would appear almost immediately.

And this made perfect sense to Santa, as how else would he be able to carry an entire supply of presents to the world's population of children in simply one night?

The chimney was a dilapidated mess, as was the rest of the home, but he ignored it. There was a child inside and that was all that mattered to him.

Sliding down the chimney, he came up in a small living room. There was a small Christmas tree in the far corner and he waddled over to it, all the time humming a holiday tune. He didn't see the talismans to the voodoo religion, nor see the dead chicken or dried crows feet dangling from a nearby alter.

No, Santa only had eyes for the Christmas tree.

So when he set the present down under the tree, he was shocked when a shadow lunged out from the darkness and at-tacked him.

What was this? No one ever attacked Santa Claus; he was wel-comed with open arms wherever he went.

But this dark man, with face drained of color and drawn vis-age, didn't seem to care who he was. Before Santa could do any-thing to protect himself, he felt the sharp pain of teeth on his left hand, right above the fingers.

Though he was always jolly, Santa roared with anger and punched the man square in the head. The attacker fell away and Santa kicked him once in the stomach for good measure. But the attacker was only down for a moment and was soon crawling toward Santa again.

Deciding there was no time for this, and if he wasn't wanted he'd just leave, Santa retreated to the chimney and scooted up it like a worm.

On the roof, the reindeer snorted impatiently, and in seconds Santa was flying off to the next house.

His hand was bleeding profusely and he wrapped it in a bright red handkerchief. After bandaging it, he tried to flex it and he winced in pain. The guy had gotten him good, that was for sure.

He went to the next house and the house after that, still having to do his duty as jolly old St. Nick. But as the hours passed, Santa began to feel feverish, something that had never happened before.

As Santa Claus, he was immortal, and age and sickness didn't affect him. But for some unexplainable reason, he felt ill.

So with sweat beading on his forehead, and his breath coming in gasps, it became harder to deliver the presents to children all over the world. But he was Santa Claus and he would continue, he had to; children everywhere were counting on him.

It happened somewhere over the Midwest of the United States.

Santa was steering the sleigh to the next city when he felt woozy, and before he knew what was happening, he passed out. The reindeer, old pros at their jobs, took the sleigh in for a landing on a nearby roof.

The roof the sleigh set down on was part of a massive, Victorian affair with ornate moldings and large picture windows. It was obvious the family living here was one of wealth.

The reindeer snuffed and snorted on the roof as Santa lay sprawled in the sleigh. This became the scene for almost ten minutes after touchdown, Santa never moving. But then Santa's right hand began to twitch and a moment later his eyes opened.

Looking around, he had no idea where he was or how he'd arrived here. And he felt weird, sort of hollow inside. There was a strange feeling in his stomach now, similar to hunger, but that didn't make any sense as he hadn't been hungry before passing out. He had been eating all night, cookies and milk mostly, but that was part of the job.

But then he realized he didn't feel sick any more, that he wasn't sweating, and that was a bonus. There was so much to do in so little time, and to get sick tonight of all nights was unthinkable.

He flexed his hand, the one with the bite, and found it didn't hurt any longer. That was also an added bonus.

Stepping out of the sleigh, he breathed in the night air, both fresh and crisp. There was a light dusting of snow across the city and he could see the blinking lights of Christmas decorations as they hung from doors and gutters of nearby homes.

Ignoring the odd feeling welling inside him, one he now felt deep in his gut, one of hunger but for what he had no idea, he reached into his magic sack and pulled out two toys. One was a train and one was a doll; then he dropped into the chimney to continue his work.

He never gave any thought to why he passed out, nor why there was no more pain in his hand, nor the odd craving in his gullet for something he couldn't put his finger on.

All that mattered was to deliver the toys to the children.

He dropped down the chimney and into the living room of the home. To his left was a large, eight foot Christmas tree, filled with red, yellow and blue blinking lights. A small angel was perched on top, its angelic face watching over the room.

Santa paused at a small table set up near the tree.

Milk and cookies were laid out for him like always, the cookies on an expensive China platter.

"Oooh, chocolate chip," he whispered as he reached out and took one. The hunger was growing inside him and the cookies should do the job nicely. But instead of enjoying the first bite, he spit it out, the chewed-up mush falling to the expensive carpet. It tasted terrible. He had to wonder if this was some sort of prank, perhaps the cookies were tainted?

Deciding that was crazy, he set the half-eaten cookie down and reached for the glass of milk.

This should settle my stomach, he thought as he began to drink. But it was like he took a sip from a bucket of sewer waste. He spit out the foul tasting liquid, wiping his mouth with his sleeve. Perplexed, but not giving it too much thought, he decided this was just an anomaly. He would have a snack at the next house, but for now he had gifts to leave under the tree.

Setting the glass down, he went to the tree, admiring his reflection in the glass ornaments. As he stared at himself, he didn't like what he saw. His face was now very pale and he had dark circles under his eyes, his forehead also looking more pronounced. Gone were the rosy cheeks, to be replaced by a bluish tint.

Once again he brushed it off as the simple distorted reflection in the ornaments. Leaning down, he set the two toys under the tree. But his left arm brushed the tree and one of the ornaments was knocked off the branch to roll across the floor. Santa turned to retrieve it, and when he bent over to pick it up, he realized he wasn't alone.

A little girl, no more than four, was standing in the doorway leading to the rear of the house. She was in red and green pajamas and wore a pretty bow around her neck. She was holding a small brown bear, the bear too, having a bow around its neck. Her hair was done up with barrettes and she was the cutest thing he'd ever seen.

"Santa?" she asked in a small, tiny voice, her big blue eyes gazing up at a holiday legend.

Santa Claus didn't know what to do; he just stared down at her.

Normally he would have hypnotized the girl then sent her off to bed. In the morning, she would have believed she'd dreamt the whole thing, but instead of doing this, he found himself looking at her like a lion to a gazelle.

She gazed up at him with those wide orbs, so young and innocent, and Santa found his mouth watering with anticipation. She looked so sweet and tender, like Grade-A veal fresh out of the slaughter house.

Before he knew what he was doing, he leaned down and picked her up, and before the girl knew what was happening, he bit into her throat, just below her chin.

The girl tried to scream of course, frightened beyond belief, but Santa Claus ripped out her larynx and began to suck at the wound like he was a dying man just out of the desert. The small feet clad in pajamas kicked back and forth, but soon they stopped moving and only hung limp.

Santa Claus fed then, tearing off large chunks of the soft, pink meat. He fed until he thought he would burst, but even then he found he was still hungry.

Dropping the carcass of the girl to the floor, he went to the back of the house where the bedrooms were located. Halfway down the hallway, there was a door with the name **Johnny** on it and he entered; another shadow amongst shadows.

Before the little boy knew what was happening, Santa Claus feasted on the little girl's brother, tearing the small form apart and feeding on the warm, juicy innards.

When he was finished he went to the parents' bedroom, killing both with teeth and fingernails. But when he began to feed, he found the taste of adult meat unappetizing and he spit it out.

No, the flesh of the children, of the innocent, was what he craved.

With his belly stuffed to the limit, he flew up the chimney and onto his sleigh. The reindeer snuffed a few times but didn't seem to pay him attention.

With a jerk of the reins, the sleigh took off to his next destination and then to every other house with children in the world.

But first he was going to the Smithfield Orphanage.

And he knew when he was finished there; Mrs. Claus was going to have to let his red suit out once more.

The father closed the book he was reading from and looked down into his daughter's eyes as she stared at him with trepidation from his lap.

Little Virginia Montrose blinked back a tear and touched the book her daddy had been reading from. "Is that really how it happened, Daddy? Is that why we board up all the windows and doors and block the chimney every Christmas Eve?"

The father nodded. "Yes, honey, that's exactly right. You see, Virginia, there really is a zombie Santa Claus, and every Christmas Eve he leaves the North Pole in search of the fresh meat of innocent children."

"So I have to hide and hope he doesn't find me?" she asked.

"That's correct, honey. It's so he can't get in and eat you. I wouldn't want to lose you to zombie Santa."

Virginia nodded, understanding. She knew there was once upon a time when Santa was a friend to children all over the world, and he would bring presents to them on Christmas Eve if they had been good. But now he was a flesh-eating zombie who fed on the innards of little children.

Father and daughter sat quietly for a time, both staring at the blinking Christmas tree in the corner of the living room. No pictures of Santa were to be found in the house, for he was all that was wrong with Christmas.

Finally, the father set his daughter down and stood up, crossing the room to unplug the lights of the Christmas tree.

Then he turned off the lighted decorations outside and every light in the house, bathing the home in darkness.

From outside, the house looked as cold and dark as the rest of the houses on the street, nay, the entire state, or better yet, the entire country.

"Now you go to bed and tomorrow it will be all over and you'll be safe for another year," he told Virginia when the house was darkened and all the barriers were checked once, then re-checked twice.

"Okay, Daddy, I love you. Merry Christmas," Virginia said and then ran off to bed. Her father sighed as he watched her leave, wishing things could be like they once were, when Christmas was a time of joy and cheer, not fear for ones children from an undead demon in a red suit and white beard.

He walked over to the chair he'd sat in with Virginia and plopped back down, only one small night light in the corner of the room to keep the darkness at bay.

On the small coffee table next to him sat a half bottle of Jack Daniels and one small shot glass. He poured himself a shot and then took a small sip. He planned on nursing the bottle, for it would be a long night of watching over his family.

His wife was already asleep, but she would be up in the morning to take over for him, just in case Santa was running behind this night and tried for one more child before the sun came up.

It had happened before, some unwary parent thinking it was over when it wasn't.

After sipping the liquor, he reached around to the back of the chair and pulled out a semi-automatic rifle. Now that Virginia was in bed, he could get ready. Flicking the selector switch to full-auto, he stared at the fireplace across the room. Though it had a sheet metal barrier across it, Santa had been known to slip past the barriers in other homes.

Curse him and his damn Christmas magic, he thought.

"Come on, Santa, I'm ready for you, you fat, dead bastard," he mumbled as he glanced at the now dark Christmas tree.

It was then that he heard, ever so softly, the ringing of sleigh bells. It was coming from outside the house, sounding like it was coming from far away, but he knew as time went by it would grow louder.

But there were many other homes to pick this night and he hoped the odds were with him that zombie Santa Claus would pass his house by.

Feeling a shiver go down his spine, he gripped the rifle more tightly.

THE END OF CHRISTMAS

Santa Claus closed the computer laptop and shook his head while taking off his thin, wire-rimmed reading glasses. He walked over to the television and stared at the screen filled with white snow.

"Still nothing, I just don't understand what's happening," he muttered under his breath.

Mrs. Claus entered the room, carrying a silver tray of milk and cookies—Santa's favorite snack.

"It's probably nothing, dear," Martha said as she placed the tray on a table beside Santa. "A solar flare or some such thing."

Santa picked up a cookie and took a bite. As crumbs fell into his white beard, he sighed. "For over a month, Martha? I highly doubt it. No, there's something wrong in the world. No phones, cable television or internet service for almost four weeks. I fear the worst."

"You said it was everywhere, right?" she asked.

He nodded. "As far as I can tell. Well, everywhere but here, and as you know, we're hidden from plain view."

"Well, dear, tomorrow night is Christmas Eve. When you head out to deliver presents to all the good little children, I guess you'll find out then what's been happening to the world."

He merely grunted in response, as he took another bite of his cookie.

Half an hour later, Santa left his small home to cross the town of Santa's Village. His destination was the main toy workshop, a warehouse located at the west side of town. This was where almost all the toys were designed and made.

The village was alive with activity as everyone rushed to finish the last toys so Santa could head out tomorrow night. Everywhere Santa looked he saw smiling faces. He nodded to a few elves as he walked, but most were so flustered with their chores they barely noticed him.

He didn't mind. While in the outside world Santa was a celebrity, loved by millions, here at Santa's Village—his home—he was just another worker—even if he was the boss.

Crossing the street, he waved to a few more elves and soon was at the warehouse.

From the outside, the building was rather plain, with snow piled five feet on all sides. Like all buildings in the village, this one was painted white.

Despite the invisibility spell that kept Santa's Village hidden from the outside world, camouflage was still necessary in case the spell ever failed.

Santa stepped through the front door and into a cacophony of busy elves. Tables were lined up throughout the warehouse, each one for an elf. Here, they fabricated toys the old fashioned way, though many of the items were flown in from outside sources by using dummy accounts and false businesses.

Loud holiday music was being blasted through hidden speakers, adding to the merriment and chaos.

The instant Santa entered the warehouse, an elf with thick black glasses appeared, standing right behind Santa.

"Hi, Santa!" the elf yelled and Santa jumped a foot into the air.

"What the…? Who?" Santa yelled as he turned and saw the elf where a moment ago there was no one. "Rufio, what have I told you about sneaking up on me?" Santa asked as he frowned at the elf who had almost given him a heart attack.

"You said not to do it," the elf replied. "But I have big news to tell you."

"Oh, and what might that be?" Santa asked.

"I just got the latest statistic report and it looks like not only are we on time, but we're ahead of schedule in manufacturing all the toys you requisitioned, Santa."

"Wonderful, that's wonderful news, Rufio. Well done. I'll have to make sure to thank everyone personally at the party when I return from my deliveries on Christmas morning."

Santa was talking about the party they had in the village every year to celebrate another successful Christmas. The entire village would relax and have fun, with food and games and joviality. But the next day they would get right back to work, for there would only be a year before the next Christmas and there was always so much to do.

"Excellent, I'll make sure to pen you in for that speech," Rufio said as he pulled a small, computer notebook out from behind his back and began typing. "Oh, Santa, any word from the outside world?" Rufio asked. "I still can't get internet service and all the lines seem to be down. I've called Tokyo to Africa, and then Ireland, but it's like the entire network is malfunctioning."

"Yes, I'm well aware of it, and have been for quite some time. At least when I leave tomorrow night, I can see first hand what's going on with communications across the globe."

"Do you think its anything serious?" Rufio asked.

Santa frowned, the gesture seemingly out of place on his usually happy, jolly visage. "I don't know, Rufio, we'll just have to wait and see when I get to the United States."

A chorus of yells filled the warehouse and Santa and Rufio looked up to see a five foot, plush teddy bear walking down the center aisle. It had an adorable face, with big button eyes and a smiling mouth. But despite this, the bear looked mad, and as the elves tried to stop it, the stuffed animal would push them away.

One elf tore off his shirt to expose a muscled upper chest, and he pulled a small knife from a hidden pocket. He placed the knife in his mouth and growled like a warrior going into battle. He climbed onto a table and jumped onto the back of the teddy bear, to then hack and slash at the fake fur.

Stuffing went everywhere as the teddy bear tried to yank the elf off, but the tiny warrior was in the center of the bear's back, and the arms wouldn't go that far. Slash after slash, the elf cut and hacked and soon the air was filled with stuffing.

The teddy bear took a few more faltering steps and then fell forward, its fluffy limbs twitching before finally remaining still.

Another elf came running up to Santa. This elf was breathing hard from the exertion of the battle and he had a small cut on his forehead. The bells on his pointed green shoes were missing, having been torn off, and his green tunic was ripped.

"I'm so sorry about that, Santa," the elf said. "Herman sprinkled too much pixie dust into the stuffing and well, you saw the result."

"Is anyone hurt?" Santa asked with a look of concern.

"No, Santa, a few bumps and bruises, but everyone's fine."

"Good, that's good. Well, tell Herman to be more careful, will you? Little Suzie doesn't want to wake up Christmas morning with a killer bear under her tree."

"Yes, Santa, right away, Santa, it won't happen again, Santa," the elf said quickly, and jogged away to help with the cleanup. Santa watched for a few seconds as the elves picked up the corpse of the teddy bear and dragged it away. A trail of stuffing was left behind, an aftermath of the toy carnage.

He turned and looked down at Rufio. "Things seem to be under control here, I think I'll go check on the reindeer."

Rufio saluted like a soldier. "Will do, Santa, just let me know if you need anything else."

Santa left the warehouse, relishing the modicum of silence as the door closed behind him.

With a heavy sigh, he let out a plume of air that coalesced into fog before him, and walked to the stables, where his cherished flying reindeer were housed.

Once more, the instant he stepped inside, an elf popped up between two bales of hay.

"Hi, Santa, what's up?"

"Oh, hello there, Marvin. I just wanted to drop by and check on the reindeer."

Marvin smiled proudly. "They're all set for tomorrow night, Santa. I've fed them and brushed them and made sure they have enough water. They'll be fed tomorrow afternoon, that way they won't be too full to fly." He chuckled at that, finding it amusing.

"Good, good, excellent. I want to see them."

"Of course, right this way." Marvin led Santa deeper into the stable until he stopped at a wide barn door. Opening it, he gestured for Santa to go first. As he did, he entered a large room the size of a three car garage. Here, the reindeer were basically lounging around, a few sitting while others stood. When they saw Santa, they all stood up and came to him. Santa reached into his pocket and pulled out a handful of oats, which he fed each of them in kind. He counted them, making sure they were all there.

"Ah, Dasher, Dancer, Prancer, Vixen, Comet, Cupid, Donner and..." He paused. "Where's Blitzen?" Santa asked.

"Huh? I don't know, he should be here," Marvin said as he counted the reindeer.

Then, from behind a small wall of hay, Blitzen appeared. He trotted over to the rest of the group and Santa patted his head. "Ah, there you are, old friend, I was worried there for a second."

Blitzen snorted like a horse and ducked his head. Santa smiled widely, letting out a loud bellow of laughter. "Ho-ho-ho! Well done, Marvin, they look fit and ready for their long journey ahead. I don't know what I'd do without them, you know."

"Take a plane?" Marvin inquired.

Santa laughed again and patted the short elf on the head, much like the reindeer. "Very funny, I highly doubt that would work as well as my reindeer do. Well, I'll be going now, I will see you boys tomorrow," he said to the reindeer as he left the stable.

All was well, or as well as it could be given his lack of communication with the outside world. At least whatever was happening hadn't affected his village.

Now that it was getting so close to departure, he had to admit he had a bad feeling deep down inside. Of course, it was possible something silly had happened. But for the entire world to go dark and cease communications, well, that couldn't bode well.

Either way, he would find out tomorrow night when he went on his yearly trek to deliver presents to good little boys and girls. Until then, he would have to wait and do what he did every year, which was to eat. He had lost some weight over the summer and had been doing his best to bulk up. After all, no one liked a skinny Santa.

Hoping Martha had baked those chocolate chip cookies she had promised earlier that morning, he headed back home to check.

"Now you be safe, dear," Martha told Santa as he finished checking his sleigh. The bright red sled was sitting outside the stable, the reindeers harnessed and ready to go. More than ten elves were all rushing about; making sure Santa was as ready to go as he possibly could. There was only one large sack in the back of the sleigh; it was all that was needed.

Using Christmas magic, the one toy sack had an infinite bottom. All Santa had to do was reach inside it and pluck out the toy he needed. After all, how else could he deliver all those toys all over the world in only one trip?

"That's a funny thing to say, Martha," Santa replied as he stepped up into the sleigh. "What makes you say that?"

"Oh, I don't know, it's just…well, we still don't know why there's a blackout across the world, and for all we know there could have been some calamity or natural disaster."

"That's silly, Martha, you're being overdramatic. If it was something like that, then we would have felt the effects here in the village, too."

"Not if it was something viral. Maybe one of those Middle Eastern countries let loose a biological agent or some awful thing."

He chuckled, his ho-ho-ho, barely a whisper. "Martha, I swear, you've been watching too many horror movies. I'm sure there is a perfectly rational explanation to whatever has happened. Now, my love, it's time for me to leave. Boys and girls everywhere are waiting for me."

She stepped close to him and kissed his cheek. "I know that, and that's why you're Santa Claus. Just promise me you'll come back in the morning, no matter what."

He sighed and with a nod, decided to humor his wife. "I promise, I'll be back, no matter what." He picked up the reins and gave them a gentle tug.

Blitzen was in the lead and when Santa gently nudged him, he snorted and began to move, causing the other reindeer to do the same. Santa circled around the stable until he was in an open clearing used for take-offs and landings, and with another tug on the reins, he let Blitzen know it was time to go.

All the reindeer began to jog, then run, and soon they were galloping across the snow-covered ice. And then, when Blitzen jumped, the others followed suit and the sleigh lifted into the air, floating on a cloud of Christmas magic.

Santa banked around the roof of the stable and with a, "Ho-ho-ho! Merry Christmas!" he flew over the village and into the clouds, soon lost from sight, the tinkling of sleigh bells wrapped around the necks of the reindeer also fading.

Martha hugged herself as she stared up into the night sky, her mouth set in a slim line. Rufio walked over to her and tugged on her apron. Looking down, she saw the elf frowning.

"You look like I feel, Mrs. Claus," he said. "Care to share why you look so worried."

She nodded slightly. "Oh, Rufio, I don't know why I feel this way. I should be happy. After all, it's Christmas Eve. But for some reason, I have this feeling of dread that I just can't shake."

"Yes, I feel it, too. It has to do with us losing communication with the outside world. Whatever the reason, it can't be good."

"I agree," she said. "I just hope he comes back to us safe and sound."

Rufio plastered a wide smile on his face, only half of it forced. "Hey, of course he will, after all, he's Santa Claus."

After crossing the ocean, Santa came in for landing in a small town in Maine. He noticed that the town was dark, which seemed odd to him. As he flew over the town square, he saw the Christmas tree was dark, where it was normally lit up, a beacon he would normally use to find the town.

This was his first stop. From here he would continue across America and then head out to other countries.

There was a small park near the first house he planned to visit and he landed in the white fluff of the light snowfall. In the wan light of the moon, the snow glistened like glass, reflecting the light as if a thousand stars had fallen to earth.

Climbing off the sleigh, he patted each reindeer in turn, the animals sniffing and growling playfully. Each reindeer was covered in a thin sheen of perspiration from the long flight from the North Pole and their breath blew out in great clouds as they exhaled.

No sooner did Santa turn and walk away, then the reindeer began to root under the light snow, searching for tender grass. Santa looked all around him, making sure it was clear. A spell of invisibility covered the reindeer, but only from sight. If a passerby stumbled into the sleigh or the animals, they would be in for quite a surprise. Thus was the reason why he landed in the park and from there would make his rounds in a large section of the town. Then he would fly to the other side and do the same there. He rarely landed on rooftops such as the stories told as there was no room. Much like an airplane, he needed room to take off and land.

With his magic sack of toys over his shoulder, he began walking to the dark house fifty feet away.

As he exited the park to cross the road, he did see one lone figure in the shadows at the end of the street. He stopped to see what the figure would do but as he watched, the figure turned and shambled away, as if he or she was drunk. What was odd was the figure didn't seem to be wearing a coat, but looked as if he or she was wearing only pajamas. Shrugging his shoulders, deciding someone was out for a late night walk and must like the cold weather, Santa crossed the street to the house.

He scurried up the side of the home like a squirrel, using his Christmas magic to make himself lighter than air. Once on the roof, he made himself thinner and down the chimney he went.

Like a ghost, he shimmied down and came out into the living room, solidifying back into himself. He smiled as he shook his arms, the feeling always leaving his entire body tingling, much like when a person's leg falls asleep to then come back to circulation with pins and needles, only minus the pain.

The room was dark as well, the lights on the tree dead. He saw presents under the tree but they looked like they had been opened already. Or perhaps an animal had gotten into them. Ribbons and wrapping paper was scattered across the floor and he had to be careful not to step in it, or the crunch would awaken the residents.

Santa reached into a pocket and pulled out his magic notebook. Whatever house he was at, the notebook would show the names, ages and what the children wanted.

He saw there were three children in this particular home. Little Maggie, who was five, little Timmy, who was eight, and Baby Suzy, who was only a few months old. He read that Maggie wanted a dolly that sang songs and Timmy wanted a new video game system—the Z BOX.

He also read that both children had been good, or had been until a month ago. Since communications had gone down, he wasn't able to update his notebook.

Santa reached into his magic toy sack and pulled out each present, placing them under the defunct tree.

He was about to leave when he heard the sound of small footsteps coming toward him. Turning around, he saw two small figures come running out of a side hallway and charge into the room. Before he could do anything, the two children were upon him, each lunging for him.

Little Timmy jumped high and latched onto Santa's right sleeve, trying to bite him. Only Santa's heavy red suit protected him from a wound. Little Maggie stayed on the floor and jumped for Santa's right boot. Her small teeth began gnawing on Santa's black boot like it was prime rib, while her tiny arms wrapped around his ankle.

"What in the name of Christmas?" Santa yelled at the two wild children who seemed to be trying to eat him, of all things. Though he would never hurt a child, he acted on instinct, too startled to think about what he was doing. Before either child could do him any damage, he plucked each one off him and tossed them to the couch a few feet away. The small bodies bounced off the cushions and rolled onto the floor. In a split second, both were on their feet again, each crouched low and growling. Timmy had material in his mouth and Santa realized it was a piece of his red suit.

Pulling a flashlight from his pocket, Santa turned it on and aimed the beam at the two tykes. He let out a gasp when he saw their faces.

Instead of two sweet visages of innocent youth, he saw two little monsters. Their eyes were sunken into their heads and their lips were pulled back on their faces, as if the skin had dried and pulled taut. Their teeth flashed in the beam of the light and their growling increased.

Santa saw both children's pajamas were covered in what looked like dried blood, and their eyes were a milky white, for all purposes void of emotion.

With a snarl and a moan, they came for him again, and he kicked out and sent them both rolling across the floor.

Not knowing what to do, fearful for the two children's well being, he broke his rule about being seen and ran deeper into the house, in search of the parent's bedroom. He found it easily enough, and with his flashlight bobbing up and down, he entered the room.

As the beam of light landed on the bed, he let out another gasp at the sight greeting him. The mother and father were there in their bed, but they weren't all there exactly.

As Santa's eyes took in the scene before him, he saw that Mom was missing her arms and Dad only had one leg. All three of his other limbs were long gone and where they had been detached looked raw and torn, as if small teeth had worried away at the meat.

Both parents had large holes in their heads, as if something had been burrowing in their skulls, searching for the tender brains within. The bed was soaked in blood, and the once white sheets were nothing but a dark brown now. Flies buzzed about and the smell knocked Santa nearly on his butt, the charnel house odor potent beyond belief.

As he stumbled away from the murder scene, and back into the hallway, he looked back down the hallway to see the two children coming for him. Looking to his left, he saw another room and he dashed into it. He realized it was the baby's room. There was a crib in the corner and he stumbled over to it. But when he pointed the beam into the crib, all he saw were raw baby parts. A tiny arm, a piece of leg, half of a foot, and something that might have been an ear, was all that lay in the crib. The sheets of the crib was also stained a dark brown, thanks to the blood drying weeks ago.

He turned when the door was forced in and the two children dashed into the room, both attacking Santa again. He used the flashlight and hit Timmy over the head, dazing the boy. When Maggie came for his leg, he kicked her away, then pushed Timmy with his free hand. Both little monsters fell into the corner. Acting fast, Santa pocketed the flashlight, and in the gloom of the room, he spun, picked up the crib and flipped it over, then used it like a cage to trap the two children. Baby parts spilled out to fall onto the floor as the two little monsters became trapped. They reached through the wooden bars of the crib, trying to reach him, but the bars were close together and they could only get their hands part way through.

Needing to catch his breath and try to make some sense to what was happening, Santa sat on the crib, thus trapping the two tykes.

Timmy and Maggie hissed and snarled as they fought like wild animals to get free.

Santa didn't get more than a few seconds respite before a shrill scream rent the night, followed by another and another after that. Though the screams sounded almost human, he knew immediately it was his reindeer.

Jumping up, he dashed out of the bedroom and into the living room. No sooner did he leave the two children, then they pushed the crib off them and ran after Santa.

But Santa was already gone, up the chimney and onto the roof.

As he climbed down the side of the house, he stopped and cast a glance over his shoulder.

In the dark house, at a window facing the street, were the two children, clawing at the glass. One managed to smash a pane but neither could climb out, as the single pane was too small. They snarled and hissed as Santa ran across the street and back to the park.

Upon entering the park, Santa stopped short, his mouth hanging open at the sight before him.

Where his eight reindeer had been waiting for him, there was now nothing but bloody carnage from end to end. As for his reindeer, they were all dead, torn apart by what seemed to be people. There had to be more than fifty people huddled around his dead reindeer, each tearing at the carcasses, chewing on the meat. Some had their heads so far inside the stomachs of the reindeer that they couldn't be seen, while others had organs hanging from mouths as they chewed and swallowed, chewed and swallowed. Many of the people had stomachs so bloated with raw meat they looked ready to burst, and Santa took a step back in horror.

"Donner, Cupid, Comet, oh God no!" he yelled, too shocked to realize that calling attention to himself probably wasn't a very good idea.

As he yelled out, every person feeding on the carcasses stopped eating and poked their heads up, much like a wild animal would do upon spotting prey.

All eyes went to Santa Claus, who with his bright red suit, stood out like a white spot on a black piece of paper.

"Uh-oh," Santa said softly as he stared at the crowd of zombies with blood covering their faces and soaking into their clothes. In the moonlight, Santa could see their eyes, and he saw the same dead look that had been in the two children's.

Crunching snow caused him to spin around, and when he did, he found another dozen or more zombies surrounding him. As he watched them come for him, he put all the pieces together and realized the reason there had been no contact with the outside world from his village was that there had been a zombie apocalypse.

Santa found he had nowhere to go, all avenues of escape cut off. His mind raced with ideas of what he should do.

He knew about zombies from when he delivered toys to Haiti, and he knew to remove the head or destroy the brain would take them down for good. But he had no weapons, only the toys in his magic sack.

A zombie lunged for him, the first in the group, and Santa jumped out of the way, the body falling to the snow. Santa kicked the ghoul in the face, sending bloody teeth to splatter the snow like red hail. He spun when another zombie came for him and he used his belly, butting the ghoul in the chest as it tried to wrap its arms around him. Like a trampoline, the ghoul snapped back and fell into the others.

Desperate for a weapon, Santa reached into his magic sack and pulled out the first thing that came to mind.

One half of a pair of women's ice skates.

The skate was black with white trim, and the blade was honed to perfection. It was suppose to be for a girl named Cindy, who lived in the next town. She wanted to be a figure skater.

Spinning the skate so that the blade pointed out, Santa used it when the next zombie came for him. This zombie was female with a red Christmas sweater on with a green Xmas tree on the front. As she lunged for Santa, he raised the skate and brought it down on her head. The skate slid into her skull like butter and he sawed it back and forth, cutting deep into the scalp and the brain within, nearly slicing her head in two. The woman dropped to the snow, all her Christmas cheer leaking out of her to soak into the snow.

Santa spun and used the skate on another ghoul, but when he whacked it in the head, the skate became stuck! Letting it go, he pushed the body away and reached into the magic sack for something else.

He came up with a handful of music CDs. Cracking the cases, he used them like mini throwing stars, adding a little Christmas magic to see them find their targets. The silver circles flew threw the air to become embedded in faces and chests. But this did nothing to stop the undead crowd and Santa went back in the sack for something else.

He came up with a hockey stick and he swung it like a madman. The blade connected with heads, and those that had muscle and tissue missing from their necks, found the hockey stick was more than a match for their weakened throats. Heads went flying and blood sprayed into the night air as Santa went to town on the undead horde.

Head after head went flying into the night until the hockey stick cracked and the tip broke off. Using it like a spear one last time, Santa jammed it into the chest of an attacking ghoul. It didn't stop the dead man but it did allow Santa a moment to reach into his magic sack and pull out another toy.

It was a toy train, the age level under three. It was made of soft plastic and had wheels that made noise when you squeezed them. Santa stared at it, wondering what he could do with it. Then he saw the pull string on the front. It was made so a child could pull it around the house, hearing the sounds it made as he did it.

Grabbing the pull string, Santa used it on the closest zombie. He wrapped it around the ghoul's neck like a garrote, then pulled it taut. String sank into dead flesh and as he used his bulk, he pushed on the zombie's back with his knee, causing the head to snap backwards and the back to arc. As the string severed the spine from the brain, the body collapsed to the snow.

More zombies surrounded him, and seen from above, he looked like one red dot surrounded by a sea of bodies.

His magic sack was pulled from his shoulder and he tried to get it back but was too slow.

As the ghouls came for him, he reached into his pockets and pulled out candy canes. Using them like small daggers, he jammed them into the eyes of the zombies. Sometimes the candy canes would go so deep that the brains would be punctured and the body would fall to the ground, but most of the time only blindness was the result.

From between the legs of the attacking horde, two smaller monsters crawled.

Little Timmy and Maggie had managed to wiggle through the broken window of their home and they were still hungry for Santa's flesh.

While Santa fought off the ghouls from on high, the two ghouls attacked from below, and Santa let out a cry as they wrapped their small arms around his legs. As he reached down to pull them off, his left sleeve rode up on his arm, exposing the pink skin of his wrist.

A geriatric zombie with a balding pate and a Christmas shirt that said, *KISS ME, I'M OLD, MERRY CHRISTMAS*, saw the opening in Santa's armor and took advantage of it. Yellow teeth sank into Santa's wrist, but not very deep and Santa barely felt the bite. When he spun to throw the kids away, the old man was knocked away also. Santa kept on fighting, oblivious to his wound.

He pushed through the undead crowd to try and break free, but there were too many! His eyes went to the zombie standing before him, one that was holding his magic toy sack!

Before the zombie knew what was happening, Santa reached out and pulled the sack back to him. Thinking of a toy he needed, he reached in and pulled out a high-powered BB gun.

It was fully loaded, and as fast as he could pump it, he shot each ghoul in the face, aiming for the eyes. It took more than one BB to put a zombie down, but when enough BBs penetrated into the brain through the eye sockets, down they went.

He exhausted his ammunition and then reached into the sack for more toys.

This time he was creative and he pulled out a large handful of firecrackers, M80's being a few of the more powerful ones.

As the zombies came for him, trying to bite, he lit the fuses and jammed the fireworks into their gaping maws.

There were muffled pops each time the firecrackers went off and a few heads exploded like a watermelon hit with a sledge-hammer as the powerful firecrackers ignited.

But though he fought the good fight, Santa knew he was losing fast. Surrounded on all sides, he knew he couldn't keep up the battle indefinitely.

He came to a section of the park that the snow was crushed flat and he reached into his magic sack and pulled out two big handfuls of glass marbles. Tossing them onto the ground, the zombies began to slip and slide as they stepped on them, some falling so hard they cracked their heads open on the ice, staining it red.

Santa tried to see over the undead crowd to find a way to escape, but there was none.

He was about to give up hope and accept his reality, when a shadow flew over him, causing him to look up.

It was Blitzen!

Santa quickly realized he was mistaken when he had seen all his reindeer killed and being eaten. With so much blood and animal parts strewn about, trying to count all the carcasses had been impossible and it was now clear that Blitzen had escaped, flying out of harm's reach.

And now he had come back for Santa.

Acting fast, Santa reached into his toy sack and pulled out two cans of silly string—yellow and pink. He sprayed these into the faces of the zombies, causing the ghouls to sputter and spit out the foul tasting foam.

Some were blinded momentarily and Santa used this as his chance to break free of the horde. Running as fast as his chubby legs would allow, he reached a small clearing in the center of the park.

Overhead, Blitzen floated down, and before the first zombie could reach them, Santa jumped onto the reindeer's back, Blitzen taking to the air once more.

As they flew high into the night sky, Santa looked below. Now, the dark town came into focus and he fully understood what it meant. As he looked on the horizon, where there should have been the lights of other towns, there was nothing but pitch darkness.

Breathing hard, Santa repositioned himself on Blitzen and said, "Let's go home, boy, there's no reason for us to stay here any longer."

With a snuff, the reindeer turned north, flew into the clouds and continued toward home.

Hours later, Santa and Blitzen arrived back at the North Pole.

Everyone gathered around, not understanding why Santa had returned so soon and why he was riding only one lone reindeer and was minus his sleigh.

Martha walked up to him and Santa kissed her on the cheek.

"It's as you feared," he told her. "It looks like there was a zombie uprising and that's the reason why the world has gone silent." He quickly filled them in on his night and what had happened to the other reindeer.

"Oh my lord, no," she said. "Those poor reindeer. Are you all right?"

He nodded, patting her arm. "Yes, yes, I'm fine. As I said, I ran into a town full of them but I managed to fend them off. But I have to be honest. If Blitzen hadn't arrived when he did, well…" he trailed off and she knew exactly what he was trying to say. She hugged him and muffled her sobs of happiness that he had returned to her.

Rufio pulled on Santa's jacket. "Santa, what are we going to do now?"

Santa shrugged. "There's nothing we can do, Rufio. The world as we know it is gone. There's no use for toys in a land of the walking dead. I guess we're out of business."

Other elves standing around them began to talk and murmur amongst themselves.

Santa raised his hands in the air to calm them. "Now, now, it's not so bad. At least we're safe here at the North Pole from whatever caused this terrible thing. We'll be fine and someday, when this is all over, we can go back to what we know and love. There's sure to be survivors."

More murmurs began and Santa quelled it once more. "That's enough for now. Tomorrow afternoon, there will be a village meeting in the main toy workshop. That's where we'll discuss what to do next. Now everyone, go back to your homes, I know for me it's been a long night and I need to rest."

Everyone began to shuffle away and Rufio pulled on Santa's jacket yet again. "Are you sure you're all right, Santa? Is there anything I can get for you? Do you need the village doctor?"

"No, Rufio, I'm fine, really, I'm just tired. I just need to sleep." Santa patted the elf on the head with a wan smile. Santa and Martha walked to their home, Martha asking question after question.

When they finally arrived home, Santa took off his blood-covered, torn red suit and went right to bed. He was so tired, which he didn't fully understand. He was immortal after all and normal ailments didn't affect him.

Martha made him a cup of hot cocoa and after he drank it he quickly he fell asleep.

He slept so heavily, some would say he slept like the dead.

As he tossed and turned, mumbling to himself about zombies and his slaughtered reindeer, the small bite on his wrist pulsed slightly as thin blue lines of infection crawled up his arm.

The next day would indeed be a memorable one for the North Pole, for in the morning, Santa would be a brand new man.

Or is that *dead* man?

EVEN ZOMBIES LOVE CHRISTMAS

Santa leaned back in his stuffed red leather chair as he read over the wish list of children all across the globe.

"One white male arm, one black left hand, one Asian right foot, a kidney from a Mexican, a spleen from an albino." He paused. "An albino? Who the hell do these kids think I am?"

Herman the elf stopped writing and waited patiently for Santa to continue.

Santa kept mumbling to himself and then stopped, scratched his beard, and looked down at Herman.

"Ready when you are, Santa."

"I lost my train of thought. Where were we?"

"An albino spleen."

"Oh yes, A spleen. I tell you, Herman, things were so much easier back when there were living people and the dead didn't rule the Earth."

Herman shrugged. "Well, we did learn to adapt, right, Santa?"

Santa sighed. "I suppose, but you have to admit, things are a lot bloodier than they were before. So, how are the human pens coming?"

"Hang, on, I'll call Sherman and check." He reached into his pocket and pulled out his cell phone. Hitting the number one for speed dial, he paused a few seconds, humming a Christmas tune as he waited.

A voice came on the other end. "Go for Sherman."

"Cut it out, answer the phone right, you idiot," Herman snapped. "Listen, I'm here with Santa, and he wants to know how the human pens are doing."

"All good, fed and watered. We're ready to start chopping them up as soon as Santa gives us the list."

Herman covered the phone with his hand and said, "Just waiting on the list, Santa."

Santa nodded. "Then let's finish this up so I can go see Melvin."

Herman spoke into the phone quickly, telling Sherman what was going on, then snapped it closed and pocketed it. Santa nodded and continued reading off the list of items, and Herman kept writing them down.

An hour later, Santa was at Melvin's cottage at the end of Santa's Village. At one time Melvin had been the tailor, but due to the change in world events, the elf was now the armorer for the village.

As Santa entered the cottage, a small bell rang over his head.

Melvin looked up from the desk he was sitting behind, a strong white light illuminating the small red orb in his hand.

"Ah, Santa, just in time. Here, let me show you what I've been working on. Follow me outside, please."

Santa followed Melvin outside and around to the back of the cottage, where the snow was churned from what looked like explosions.

The two stopped by a four foot wall of ice and snow.

Melvin held up the orb so Santa could see it. "My new invention, an Ornament grenade." He handed it to Santa, who studied it.

"Well, I can see why you call it an Ornament. It looks just like the ones hung off of Christmas trees."

Melvin gestured to the top of the grenade, where there was the typical loop for where a hook would go for hanging. "Exactly. Now slide your finger in the loop and pull."

Santa did as he was told. "And?"

Melvin's eyes went wide. "And throw it, Santa! Throw it!"

"Whoops," Santa said and tossed the ornament downrange, where it landed and erupted a second later, sending a shower of ice and snow in all directions.

Melvin and Santa closed their eyes as the wave subsided, hiding behind the ice wall.

"Not bad, Melvin, not bad, but you know, you didn't need to make it look like an ornament. A simple grenade would have been fine."

Melvin shrugged. "Traditions die hard with me, Santa. I know things have changed for the worse, but we can still try to hold on to the old ways."

"If only that were true, Melvin," Santa agreed as the elf led him back inside, talking the entire time.

"I have a whole new arsenal for you to take with you this year, Santa," Melvin said as they entered the cottage and closed the door. Melvin waddled over to a bench stacked with what looked like harmless items. "Here, come take a look."

Santa shuffled over and examined the array of items. He spotted a few sugar cookies and he reached down and picked one up. It was in the shape of a star, and as he opened his mouth to take a bite, Melvin grabbed his arm and shouted, "No, don't eat that!"

"Why not? Melvin, I'm Santa, I love cookies."

"Yes, Santa, but that's not a real cookie. Here, give it to me, let me show you."

Santa handed him the sugar cookie and Melvin held it in his hand and turned to face the far wall, where Melvin then pointed. Santa let his eyes go to the wall and saw there were numerous indents in the plaster, like something sharp had been thrown into it; like a knife.

Melvin pulled back his arm and threw the cookie like it was a baseball. The cookie sliced through the air and ended up sticking in the wall by one of its points.

Melvin smiled. "See? It's modeled after a Ninja star. Perfectly balanced. You can throw it any which way and it always soars true and finds its target."

Santa frowned. "So you're saying there aren't any cookies to eat?"

Melvin looked at Santa like he was an idiot. "No, there aren't any cookies."

"Okay then, I'll have some of this cocoa," Santa said and reached for the open plastic thermos next to the sugar cookies/throwing stars. He picked the thermos up, and was about to take a sip when Melvin yelled, "No, wait, stop!"

Santa had the thermos half tipped back and all he had to do was move his arm a little bit more to pour out the chocolately goodness. He held his arm in place and looked at Melvin. "What now?"

"Santa, please, carefully hand me that hot cocoa and I'll show you. But be very careful you don't spill any on yourself."

"Why the hell not?"

"Santa, please just trust me, all right?"

Santa sighed and did as he was told, and a second later Melvin was holding the thermos of hot cocoa.

"There, good, wow, that was a close one. Here, let me show you what this really is." He walked over to a small statue of a snowman and poured some of the hot cocoa onto the top of its head. When the dark liquid hit the statue, the snowman began to hiss and melt.

Santa swallowed hard, imagining the liquid going down his throat. "What is that?"

"Hydrochloric acid that smells and looks like hot cocoa."

"Acid? Now why in all that's holy would you go and make it smell like…" Santa stopped and composed himself, realizing who he was dealing with. "You know what? Never mind, it doesn't matter."

Melvin smiled and walked over and put the cap on the acid, then handed Santa a large candy cane about the size of a walking stick.

"What's this, a throwing spear?" Santa asked sarcastically.

Melvin smiled. "You're getting the hang of it but no, it's not a spear." He gestured to the top where the cane curved. "Turn that and pull."

Santa did as he was told and a second later was holding a long sword the length of the cane.

"Now this I like," Santa said with a smile and waved it around.

"Toledo steel from Spain," Melvin bragged. "Will take a head off like…well, like a hot blade through butter."

Santa slid the sword back into the sheath and smiled. "What else do you have for me?"

Melvin showed Santa a few more clever items, such as smaller candy canes that worked as nun-chucks when they were attached or individually as daggers, the points sharp enough to pierce the skull of a human. He also had the standard firearms, such as pistols and revolvers, shotguns and machine guns and a few Uzis. Everything a Santa on the go would need as he made his rounds in an undead world.

"Good, good, it all looks wonderful. Melvin, my boy, you've outdone yourself this year."

"Thanks, Santa. I have to admit, this is a lot more fun than making your red and white suits."

"Well, it shows, it certainly does. Have all this stuff sent to the sleigh and I'll be ready come tomorrow night for Christmas Eve."

"Will do, Santa, you can count on me."

Santa left the elf armorer and headed across the village. Mrs. Claus was working on his suit and he was looking forward to what she'd done to it.

Mrs. Claus was busy working when Santa entered their home on the north side of the village. As he entered, she looked up, a wide smile on her face.

"There you are, and just in time, I'm about done with your new suit."

"And how's it coming?" he asked, joining her and giving her a kiss on the cheek.

"Very well, the leather was a bit tough to sew but I managed."

"Leather? On my suit? Really?"

"Of course, dear," she said. "Remember what happened last year? You were nearly bitten and it was sheer luck that old man had no teeth in his mouth. If he'd died with his dentures in, why, you wouldn't be here today!"

He had to admit she was right. He'd been in a nursing home delivering presents when an old man had come out of the shadows. The old zombie must have been in his eighties when he'd died and returned, and before Santa could react, the old man sank his teeth into his arm — or tried to. But the zombie was tooth-less, and other than leaving behind a trail of bloody spittle, Santa had been unharmed. He'd caved in the zombie's skull and got out of there before any others had seen him.

"That was a close one, wasn't it," he mused.

"It sure was. So I made sure something like that can never happen again. Here, have a look at what I've done to your suit."

He stepped closer to see his red and white suit was on a mannequin. He grunted a little in annoyance when he saw how fat the mannequin was. It made him uncomfortable. Though he'd always been rotund, he'd also always been sensitive about his weight. He played his eyes over the suit, admiring his wife's handiwork. She was an excellent seamstress and her skill showed in the fine stitching.

The suit was still red and white, only now it had touches of black leather as well. The arms and legs were completely encased in thick leather, as were the shoulders. A lightweight wire mesh surrounded the main torso and the belt was made of copper with a small, two inch knife hidden within the emblem of Santa on his sleigh. As he studied the suit, it reminded him of what gladiators in Greece wore when entering the arena in battle.

"Go on, dear, try it on for size. I just finished before you arrived."

"Okay, will you give me a hand?"

She nodded and helped him slide the suit off the mannequin, then helped him dress. Moments later he was wearing his new suit and he had to say it fit pretty well. It was heavier of course, but the leather was supple. As he walked around the room, he squeaked a little, the leather being broken in.

She frowned at the squeaking. "I'll see what I can do about it but I may not be able to stop it."

"I'll deal with it," was all he said as he waddled across the living room, bending and stretching to limber the leather.

"Did you see Melvin?" she asked.

"Yes, he has a full arsenal for me."

"Good, I want to know you can defend yourself if you have to," she said.

He walked over to her and kissed her again. "No worries there. One thing's for sure. Tomorrow night when I make my rounds, the living dead will find me a hard nut to crack."

The sun was just beginning to set as Santa Claus left the village behind and began his trek to the real world—or what was left of it.

Behind him, in his magic bag, were all the items from the wish list. The bottom of the bag was soaked with congealed blood and flies could be heard buzzing within it. Santa was just glad he was in the open air and the stench of body parts was lost in the wind.

For the thousandth time he wondered if what he was doing was right. Of course he knew it was wrong to kill the humans in the pens at the village, but he really had no choice. He was Santa Claus after all. His job was to fulfill the wish lists of children all over the world. Only now, the undead children didn't want bicycles, ponies or choo-choo trains. They wanted arms, legs and internal organs to feed on.

It was a new world and he either adapted to it or would die out. He may have been around for centuries but that was only because he was needed by the children. If they stopped needing him…why, for all he knew he would simply grow old and die. Or worse, fade away into nothingness. He'd really never thought about it much, and who would? Why contemplate your own existence and lack thereof?

No, better to do his job, no matter how macabre it might be now.

But that didn't mean he would let them use him as a human buffet. Oh no, he may have to deliver them body parts once a year but he'd be damned if he'd let them eat him too.

So where once he would simply drop down chimneys and leave presents under trees—the only danger that of being seen by some insomniac child—now he had to worry about being attacked by the undead homeowners, who were looking for a midnight snack.

Time passed and soon he arrived at his first home in the United States. He wanted to get the US over with first before going on to other countries. Out of all the places on Earth, the US was hit the worst when the dead began to rise. As far as Santa knew, there were no other human beings left alive in the world, with the exception of the ones at his village, and they were kept for only one very gruesome thing.

Luckily, if you took a man's leg or a woman's arm, it didn't mean they were dead, but could go on for years with the missing limb as long as they were cared for and the severed limb was taken correctly. For the limbs and organs had to be fresh or the dead wouldn't eat them.

Pulling on the reins of the reindeer, Santa steered for the first rooftop he came to. It was a ranch-style house with a three-car garage and a large swimming pool in the backyard. Of course, the pool now looked more like a swamp, with a few rotting bodies floating in the muck that was once clean water, and half the garage had been burned in a long-ago fire, and the grass of the front and rear lawn was more than three feet tall and had fallen over onto itself.

It had been years since the dead began to walk and the world collapsed, and in all that time, Santa had stayed at the North Pole, only coming out once a year like always. When he thought about the first year he'd gone out and found nothing but death…well, he tried not to think about it too much. It was too hard to bear.

As the sleigh settled on the roof, he climbed out and stretched. Then he checked his list for what this house had asked for. One white right arm and a black penis, complete with testicles. He blinked and took another look to make sure he'd read it right. Then with a shrug, opened the bag of parts and began digging.

Moments later he found what he needed and prepared to enter the home.

This was one of the tricks Santa used magic for, one of the few. There was only so much magic to go around so he had to use it sparingly. He used it for mainly three things. To go down and then up the chimney, and the third was too keep his gift bag bottomless. How else could he carry all the presents in one trip?

His nose wrinkled from the smell of rotting meat as he appeared in the living room. Though he was used to the odor enough that he didn't gag, it was still hard to accept fully.

There was a Christmas tree in the corner, a fresh pine by the looks of it, but instead of tinsel and ornaments made of glass or plastic, the tree was decorated with intestines and fingers, as well as a few eyeballs. On the top of the tree, instead of a star or an angel, a severed head looked out, only the eye sockets were empty, gaping black holes.

On the table near the chimney was a plate and a glass, but where once cookies and milk would be waiting for him, now the plate held a kidney and pieces of intestines; what the owners of the home thought Santa would like to eat.

Oh, how wrong they were.

Wanting to finish up and move on to the next house, he quickly laid the body parts under the tree and was about to leave when he heard footsteps come from behind him. He looked up to see two zombie children standing in the doorway.

With a hiss and a groan they were on him, small mouths biting and snapping as they tried to feed on Santa. Lucky for him, their teeth couldn't penetrate his new suit and it was simple to toss each child off him where they landed on the couch across the room.

"Merry Christmas," he said quickly and was gone before the children could attack again, back up the chimney in a flash. Once on the roof, he listened at the opening to the chimney as the two zombie kids gnashed and moaned from below. Santa shook his head at the thought of only a few million more homes to go before he could call it a night.

Climbing onto his sleigh, he flew off into the darkness, his destination the next house on his list.

Hours later he was still going strong. He'd had a few close calls but nothing he couldn't handle. He was in the Midwest, in some town he would forget the second he left it. Landing on the roof, he slipped down the chimney, his mind already thinking of the next delivery.

As he appeared in the living room, he found he was surrounded by seven zombies, all with different rates of decay. One was so rotted it was nothing but skin and bones, the organs within its torso desiccated to the point they were useless.

The second Santa appeared, they lunged for him, teeth gnashing and fingers clawing at him, the tap sprung. One got a good grip on his long beard and only a punch to the face could get the ghoul off him.

Acting fast, Santa reached behind his back and pulled out a set of candy canes, each with a sharpened point. With one in each hand, he jabbed them into the eyes of two zombies, the points slicing into their brains and killing them instantly.

With a gap in the advancing line of zombies, he dashed through it and came up short at the opposite end of the room. Turning, he pulled out two ninja sugar cookie stars and threw them at another zombie. One cookie struck its face right below the left eye, but the second one hit paydirt, slicing through the skull and into the brain. The ghoul dropped to the blood-soaked carpet, dead.

Not having the patience for any more combat, Santa reached into his pocket and pulled out an Ornament grenade. Pulling the pin, he tossed it at the zombies with a, "Merry Christmas, ass-holes!"

The zombie in the center caught the grenade like it was a ball and looked at it with curiosity. It could see its reflection in the shiny red coating of the grenade and was fascinated.

Meanwhile, Santa dived behind a ratty couch and the entire home shook on its foundation. Bloody parts and gore flew in every direction, the walls becoming an original Jackson Pollock.

Poking his head up over the couch, he saw more than half the zombies were down. Taking his chance, he dashed to the chimney opening, and as the ghouls began climbing to their feet to renew the attack, Santa let out a laugh and yelled, "Sorry, fellas, but I'm not on the menu tonight. See you next year!" Then he was up the chimney and on the roof once more.

Later, with the United States finished, he landed on his first roof in London. It was an orphanage.

There was no chimney so he had to use the front door. It was locked but a little Christmas magic soon had him inside.

As he walked through the foyer and down a short hallway, he soon found himself in a wide open room similar to a hospital ward. Bunk-beds lined each side of the room, a thin walkway down the middle. At the end of the path was the Christmas tree. This one was old, the pine needles having fallen off years ago. The air was rank with death, but Santa swallowed the bad taste in his mouth and began walking to the tree.

When he was halfway there, he heard movement to his left, then his right, then from behind. Pulling a flashlight from his pocket, he shined it on the cause of the noise, and when he did, his heart lodged in his throat.

Undead children, more than two dozen, were coming out from under the beds and the shadows.

This had happened to him before, unfortunately, and so far he'd always managed to escape in one piece. Some zombies wouldn't settle for what he delivered them, but instead wanted to feast on his fat ass.

"Now, now, kids, let's not do this. I have some presents for you," he said and reached into his bag and tossed a few kids some bloody body parts. They grabbed them off the floor and began to feed on them, but the rest still kept coming for him.

He began to back away, but already his retreat was cut off by more undead cherubs. He was trapped.

With a low hiss, a little blonde girl with sunken-in features charged at him and he kicked her in the chest, sending her sprawling away. Then more jumped into action, charging at him, their small hands curved into claws, their mouths open in anticipation of the kill.

A small boy tried to jump on his back. Santa pulled the thermos of hot cocoa from his pocket, and with lightning speed, whipped off the top. He splashed the hot cocoa smelling acid on the boy's face, who hissed in anger. The small zombie fell to the floor, his eyes melting, his face sloughing off, the flesh turning into a puddle of goo, the tongue dissolving, the teeth sliding out. The boy kept twitching until the acid finally ate into his brain and killed him.

Acting fast, Santa reached over his back and retrieved the Uzi he'd had hung there for just such an occurrence.

"Merry Christmas, you little dead bastards!" he screamed and squeezed the trigger, sending steel-jacketed rounds into the small bodies again and again. Heads exploded, limbs were chewed off, and legs were crippled, blood and gore flying in all directions. The main line of children was quickly chewed up and it made a clear hole for Santa to use.

Jumping over the first body, he ran for the door, shooting as he ran. More zombie kids were taken down as he fired.

His clip ran dry and there was no time to reload, so he let the Uzi fall from his hands to hang on its strap, then pulled a Glock from inside his suit.

As a small boy came at him, he shot the kid at point blank range, blowing out the back of the boy's head in a spray of brown and yellow brain matter.

When he reached the door, Santa stopped and turned around. The children were crawling and limping towards him, some too wounded to move.

"There's a reason you little bastards didn't have parents before you died!" he yelled, angry at himself for even saying it but getting tired of always being the blue plate special.

In reply, the zombie kids hissed and growled at him. Santa pushed through the door and locked it behind him, then made his way back to the roof. Despite this and other setbacks, he still had a long night ahead of him.

That was okay; he also had a full load of ammunition as well.

By the time he was finished for the night and had returned to the North Pole, he was exhausted.

He'd had countless battles with the dead as the night had progressed but his wits and weapons had seen him through unscathed. His new suit had a lot to do with it as well.

There were many places where teeth marks could be seen on the leather and actual teeth were lodged in the metal mesh over his chest and back, but not one got through and touched his soft flesh beneath.

After making sure the elves in the stable were taking care of his reindeer, he made his way back home and his waiting wife.

When he entered, her eyes lit up with relief and Santa saw that she wasn't alone. Herman and Melvin were with her, no doubt keeping her company till he returned.

"I'm home," he said as he entered the house and she ran into his arms for a kiss. "Now, now, not too close or you'll get blood on you," he told her, his suit covered in zombie gore.

"I don't care, I'm just glad you're home and safe for another year."

He patted her shoulder and then extricated himself from her loving embrace. "I need to get out of this thing, it's killing me," he said and began to shrug out of the suit. "You two, give me a hand, will you please?"

Herman and Melvin did as requested and a few minutes later, Santa was standing in the middle of the living room in nothing but his red long-johns.

"How did the new suit work out?" Mrs. Claus asked.

"I have to tell you, the suit worked marvelously," he told his wife. "I can't imagine ever having done tonight without it."

"I'm so glad to hear it," she said. "In fact, I have a few more ideas for next year. How about a helmet and gauntlets and oh, what about a shield and…"

"Later, you can tell me later," he cut her off. "For now I just want to sit down and have something warm to drink."

"Here are your slippers, Santa," Herman said and slid the slippers on his feet as Santa dropped down in his favorite chair by the fire. To the right of him a beautiful pine Christmas tree brought back from the real world blinked with colorful lights. But only the standard red, blue and green ornaments on this one—no body parts at all.

Melvin went off to the kitchen and came back a minute later with a steaming mug. "Here, Santa, I made this just for you."

Santa took the mug and sniffed. It was hot cocoa. He gave Melvin a stern look and Melvin nodded and said, "Yes, Santa, it's real cocoa."

He hesitantly sipped it, and after he swallowed the first mouthful and his throat wasn't being eaten out from the inside, he began drinking it with gusto.

"How did my weapons work out, Santa?" Melvin asked eagerly.

Santa let out a hearty laugh and patted the small elf armorer on the shoulder. "They were excellent. Couldn't have been better. Thank you again, Melvin, you probably saved my life more than once because of your inventions." He winked. "And the guns didn't hurt either."

"That's so great to hear," Melvin said. "Because while you were gone, I was still working and I came up with even more great ideas. How about fig pudding that's really Semtex or tinsel that can be used as a garrote, or a stuffed animal that can be used as containers for nerve gas; just pull off the head and toss it. And…"

"Okay, okay, enough, please, not now. There's plenty of time for all that tomorrow." Santa finished his cocoa and handed the empty cup to his wife, who took it with a warm smile. "One thing I've learned since the dead began to walk is that we have all the time in the world."

"Amen to that, dear," Mrs. Claus said. "And Merry Christmas to you."

Santa smiled, his cheeks puffing up as he let out a hearty, "Ho-Ho-Ho. Thank you, dear. It's nice to have someone say it to me for once!"

Herman began to chuckle and Melvin joined in, and soon they were all laughing.

The dead may rule the Earth and death and decay were everywhere, but here, at the North Pole, life still flourished…and so did Christmas.

A YEAR WITHOUT A ZOMBIE SANTA CLAUS

"Vixen looks terrible," Santa Claus said as he stared at the small reindeer. He was wearing a red three-piece suit with a matching hat—he was in disguise. He hadn't wanted to leave the North Pole but when the elves Jingle and Jangle Bells had left to go to the cruel, real world with little Vixen, he had no choice. And looking at the small, sick reindeer, he knew his assumption was correct.

Vixen was lying inside a cage at the Southtown, USA Dog Pound.

"Is it the heat?" Jingle asked, his sidekick Jangle Bells—slightly taller but also slightly slower in intelligence—standing beside him with concern written all over his face. Both wore red outfits, and looked very out of place in the southern state that had had no snow in years.

"I suppose so," Santa said as he opened the cage door and picked up the small, shivering reindeer. He didn't notice the small bite mark on Vixen's right, rear leg. The bite had occurred shortly after Vixen had been captured by the dog catcher and taken to the pound. She had been in a cage with another dog and this dog had been diseased. It never should have happened, but the dog catcher wasn't the most caring man and he had wanted to go to lunch, so had simply tossed the little reindeer with socks on her head to cover her small ears and budding horns—so she looked like a dog…it was Jingle's idea—into the cage. Vixen had curled up in the corner but the dog had growled menacingly, and before Vixen could react, the dog had lunged and bit her on the leg. No doubt the dog would have probably killed Vixen if not for the dog catcher reconsidering his decision moments later and instead taking Vixen and putting her in her own cage.

But the damage was done; the bite had transferred the disease the dog had been carrying, whatever it was. Rabies, some kind of exotic disease, it was never known as no veterinarian examined the sick animal.

The dog had died an hour after biting Vixen and was carried to the back of the pound, where the incinerator was located. As the door had closed on the still carcass, and the flames began to lick out at the body, the dog's eyes had snapped open and it began to howl as the dead carcass began to reanimate.

But before so much as one howl could escape the fire pit, the flames consumed it and destroyed the abomination.

"Come on, girl, let's get you home," Santa said to Vixen as he cradled the small reindeer in his arms. Vixen's eyes were closed and her chest heaved slightly as she struggled to breathe. The socks had been removed from her head and the dog catcher was staring, amazed at the thought of a real live reindeer in his pound. He said as much but Santa only nodded. He wasn't here to get people to love Christmas, he was here to bring home his sick reindeer.

"You two boys are coming home, too," Santa said to Jingle and Jangle.

"But, Santa," Jangle said, "what about us finding out about the spirit of Christmas?"

"That doesn't matter any more, boys, we need to get Vixen home. Now, I called Maw and she's on her way to pick you both up, then we'll all fly home together."

"Mrs. C is coming here?" Jangle asked.

Santa nodded as he began to leave the pound, Jingle and Jangle right behind him. "That's right, and as soon as she arrives, off you go back home."

The dog catcher watched the curious group of people leaving: a rotund old man with a white beard, a reindeer, and two dwarves, all wearing red. Scratching his head, he got back to work.

Once outside, Santa and the elves walked around to the back of the building, where Blitzen was waiting for Santa. Blitzen had carried Santa from the North Pole and he didn't like the heat at all. He desperately wanted to go back home. When Blitzen saw Santa carrying Vixen, he began to shake his head, saddened that one of his kind was ill.

"Don't worry, Blitzen," Santa said. "Once we get home, we'll get Vixen better."

Blitzen only nodded in response, shifting a front hoof across the ground. They didn't have to wait long for Mrs. Claus, as Santa had called her before entering the dog pound after he'd met up with Jingle and Jangle.

She was in a small sleigh, only large enough for her ample frame and one adult passenger, or two elves, which were about the same width.

Dasher was attached to the sleigh and pulled Mrs. Claus through the air, and gently touched down before Santa and the elves. Santa walked over to his wife of many years and kissed her softly on the cheek.

"It's good to see you, Maw."

"And you as well, dear." Her eyes fell on Vixen and her face sank with worry. "Oh no, will you look at her. The poor thing, we need to get her home."

"I couldn't agree more," Santa said and turned to look down at Jingle and Jangle Bells. "You two get into the sleigh with Maw. We're leaving this place right now."

Jangle looked like he was going to protest but Jingle touched his shoulder and shook his head, telling his brother elf not to say a word. Jangle heeded the warning and simply climbed into the sleigh, getting close to Mrs. Claus as Jingle also got in.

Santa nodded, glad his order was being followed without compromise, then he climbed onto Blitzen and the reindeer began to run before leaping into the air, flying high over the town. Mrs. Claus gave a light snicker and Dasher heeded her order and began to run, then leaped as well, taking the sleigh into the air. In seconds, the two flying objects quickly began to grow small in the sky. If any of the townspeople saw flying reindeers overhead, none admitted it later.

"Be careful now, boys," Mrs. Claus said. "We're flying into Snow Miser's territory."

"He almost got us last time we went through here with Vixen, Mrs. C," Jingle said as he peered over the side of the sleigh. He could see nothing but clouds, white and puffy.

"Ah, Maw," Santa said, flying beside her on Blitzen. "It's late in the day; I doubt he's keeping watch."

Suddenly, a blinding ray of freezing water and ice shot up out of the clouds and struck the back of the sleigh. It bucked terribly and Jangle would have fallen out if Jingle hadn't grabbed his brother elf and yanked him back on his seat.

"Oh dear, we're hit!" Mrs. Claus screamed as the sleigh began to go into a spin. Dasher let out a grunt and tried to keep the sleigh airborne but one of the struts had been hit and it was causing the sleigh to wobble like a toy top coming off the elf assembly line all warped. For the sleigh needed to be aerodynamic to help keep it aloft. Try as he might, he wasn't able to accomplish this task and he and the sleigh began to tailspin into the clouds.

"Maw!" Santa yelled and directed Blitzen to follow the falling sleigh. The clouds surrounded them all as Santa tried desperately to catch his falling wife, but she was moving too fast. He feared the worst when suddenly, a giant mound of snow appeared through the clouds, and the sleigh, Mrs. Claus and the two elves, along with Dasher, all landed heavily but safely in the powdery substance, disappearing from sight as they sank into the mound.

Santa steered Blitzen over the mound of snow and landed on its outer edge, Vixen still cradled in his arms. The small reindeer was sleeping. As for his wife and the elves, there was no sign.

"Maw! Maw! Where are you? Are you all right?" He wondered what he could do to help. Trying to dig her out seemed foolhardy and though he was Santa Claus, he wasn't a god. He might be immortal but his Christmas magic only went so far.

He was still pondering all this and thinking he should head back to the North Pole for help when the snow began to shake and shimmer near him. A second later, the two elves stepped out of the snow, followed by Dasher and then, finally, to Santa's relief, Mrs. Claus.

"Oh, thank the Maker," Santa said and went to his wife, hugging her. "I was so worried; I didn't know what to do."

"I'm fine, dear," Mrs. Claus said. "We all are. This pile is as soft as a cloud and as fluffy as new-fallen snow. We were able to simply walk through it, as if it was nothing more than a thick cloud."

"What a ride," Jingle said. "My heart was in my throat. I had to swallow it back down."

Jangle only nodded.

Jingle then turned around and went back into the snow mound, coming out backwards a second later. He was dragging the sleigh. "Hey, give me a hand, you lazy elf," he said to Jangle. "This thing is heavy." Jangle went and helped and the two elves continued to drag the sleigh free of the snow, a lot of huffing and puffing the result. When they finally had it clear, everyone took a good look at it.

"Oh dear, that won't be flying anytime soon," Mrs. Claus said as she examined the sleigh.

"What I want to know is what happened," Santa added.

"I think I can shed some light on that one, fatso," a voice said from behind them. The group all turned as one to see none other than Snow Miser coming towards them, an entourage of his two foot tall minions that were identical to him in every way—right down to their scarves and attire, only much smaller—right behind him.

"Snow Miser," Mrs. Claus said, her mouth falling open. "It was you who brought my sleigh down."

"Of course it was, madam. Who else would it be?" He sidled over to her and put an arm around her ample shoulders. She cringed but held her ground. "So tell me, my little icicle," he said, "when are you gonna leave old fatso over there and come and live with me?"

She brushed off the arm from her shoulder, as if it was the most detestable thing she had ever come in contact with. "Never, and I've told you that before."

"Oh come, come, Mrs. C, I can give you so much more than this old fart ever could."

"I'm standing right here, you know," Santa said, staring at Snow Miser with what looked like anger—though Santa was supposed to be always jolly, even he had his breaking point—and Snow Miser was it.

Next to his brother Heat Miser, Snow Miser was the worst, though the two siblings fought terribly. Snow Miser wanted snow and his brother Heat Miser always wanted it hot.

"Yes, I know, tubby," Snow Miser quipped. "And I don't care." He clapped his hands and the little entourage of Snow Misers jumped to attention. "You guys take Mrs. Claus' sleigh and get it fixed up for her." The little ones did as they were told. Snow Miser turned back to Mrs. Claus with a wide smile that resembled a fox after it had gotten inside the hen house. "And you, Mrs. C, will stay for the night till your sleigh is fixed. You'll be my honored guest."

"What about us?" Santa asked, not liking being left out of the conversation. He was Santa Claus after all and he was being treated like a second-rate citizen by Snow Miser.

"Huh?" Snow Miser said, as if just noticing Santa was there for the first time. He waved his hand at Santa and the elves. "Yes, yes, I suppose you can stay, too."

Snow Miser walked over to Santa and stared him down. "You're lucky I'm in a good mood, fatso, or else I'd ship you home in a block of ice." As he said this, he was poking Santa with his right index finger, each word followed by a jab into Santa's chest.

Vixen woke up and saw the hand over her head and couldn't resist. She didn't understand why, but for some reason she was craving flesh, and even Snow Miser's cold flesh would do in a pinch. Before anyone could stop her, Vixen lunged up in Santa's arms and sank her sharp teeth into Snow Miser's right wrist.

"Yow!" Snow Miser yelled and yanked his arm back, a good-sized chunk of flesh now gone from his wrist. Vixen chewed thoughtfully as she stared at Snow Miser.

"What the blue blazes is wrong with that animal, fatso?" He was cradling his arm. "Put that thing in a muzzle!"

Santa was as shocked as Snow Miser but he had to admit that when he considered it, he really wasn't too upset. He did pull Vixen back from Snow Miser, and when she tried to bite Santa, too, he had to adjust her so her neck was under his arm, her head sticking out so that if someone was standing behind Santa, they would see his back and Vixen's head protruding from between his arm and body.

Snow Miser was examining the wound, frowning. It was bleeding slowly, but as soon as the blood seeped from the wound, it froze up and dropped to the ground as red ice crystals.

"Stupid reindeer," Snow Miser mumbled. "I oughtta make hamburgers out of you."

Mrs. Claus walked over to Snow Miser and held out her hand. In her other one was a handkerchief. "Here, Snowy, let me see that," she said, her voice one of a caring mother.

Snow Miser melted when she said it and he held out his hand like a small child, his lower lip quivering. "It really stings," he said, his voice high-pitched.

Mrs. Claus examined it and nodded to herself, then wrapped it up with the handkerchief, tucking in the loose end under a fold. "There, all better. It's just a small cut, you'll be fine. Though you need to make sure you clean it good."

"I will, Mrs. C, thank you," Snow Miser said, then he flashed Santa Claus an evil stare. "I want that animal on a leash from here on out. You got me, fatso?"

Santa sighed, too tired to want to duel with Snow Miser. "Yes, I understand."

Snow Miser clasped his hands, then winced and regretted it. "Minions, take Mrs. Claus to a room for the night, and the others as well."

The little versions of Snow Miser all nodded and ran over to Mrs. Claus and the elves, taking them by the hand and leading them away.

Santa stood alone as everyone was moving away and he cleared his throat and said, "Uh, what about me?"

Snow Miser turned and glanced back at Santa. "Oh, sorry, tubby, I forgot about you. It's so easy to do. I swear, you're as memorable as a cup of water in the ocean. Follow me. I have a *special* room for you."

Santa didn't like the sound of that but he said nothing. With Vixen fighting him as she struggled to get free, Santa followed the others, while behind him, more of the Snow Miser's minions got to work dragging the sleigh away to get it fixed and also to get Blitzen and Dasher fed and stabled.

Santa looked around his room, frowning as the second airplane in as many minutes flew by. Snow Miser had put him in a room at the very end of his airborne complex and it seems it was right on the fly-by route of a local airline.

So much for getting any rest, Santa thought with a deep frown.

He placed Vixen in a corner of the room, on a wadded-up blanket and patted her head gently. This time she didn't try to bite him. "Hang in there, girl, we'll be home soon." Santa stared at the reindeer as she curled up and went to sleep. He didn't understand the way Vixen was acting. Now that they were long gone from Southtown, the heat had abated and she should have been recovering. And the biting of Snow Miser was even more unusual. Vixen had never showed a bad bone in her body, and was the gentlest of creatures, so the biting was very unlike her. But Santa couldn't find too much fault in her for doing it. Hell, he had wanted to take a bite out of Snow Miser on more than one occasion over the years. Snow Miser was always hitting on Martha and though he hated to admit it, Santa was jealous.

He let his eyes play over the room, taking in the modest furnishings, all made out of ice. Well, the host was called Snow Miser after all, a magical entity who could harness the power of snow and at the snap of a finger could make it snow anywhere in the world—or never snow there if that was the choice.

There was a fireplace in the corner and a roaring fire was already going, but heat didn't affect the ice furniture—magic again.

Santa slid out of his suit and put it on a hanger, then slid into bed, exhausted. His cold wasn't much better and every bone in his body ached.

He expected the bed to be warm and comfortable, for despite being made of ice, magic should have made it cozy and snug, but the bed was freezing. He frowned so deeply it was a miracle his mouth remained on his face. Snow Miser had taken the magic from the bed so Santa would have a terrible night's rest. But Santa had some magic of his own and it wasn't long before the bed was the way a bed should be, warm and snuggly.

Of course, the planes flying by couldn't be helped, but Santa was so doggone tired that he barely heard the next one as he drifted off into a heavy sleep, snoring loudly.

Curled up near his bed, Vixen's chest rose and fell, rose and fell, until finally in the middle of the night, she stopped breathing. As the reindeer succumbed to the virus sweeping through her frail body, her bladder and bowels voided in death, seeping into the blanket. The room shook as another airplane soared by.

While Santa, Mrs. Claus, and the elves lay sleeping, Snow Miser was tossing and turning in his massive ice bed, carved from a giant block of ice; he seemed lost in the large bed.

His face was creased in pain as something amazing began to happen to him. Vixen's wound had festered and now, the virus was doing its best to take over his frigid body.

But Snow Miser wasn't human, he was magical, and the virus mutated because of this, still taking over Snow Miser's body but leaving his intellect intact. As he sweated ice cubes and shivered as if he was cold, the virus filled every cell, every nerve ending, until Snow Miser was no more, and instead, an undead entity took his place.

The next morning, Snow Miser's eyes snapped open and he got up and went to the ice mirror near his bed. Gazing at the gaunt face looking back at him, he saw he was paler than he'd ever been—and that was saying something! He flexed his hands, feeling how different they felt, how *he* felt.

Then he realized something. He wasn't breathing. Normally, when he exhaled, his breath came out looking like steam—though he was the master of snow, he was still a living creature.

But now…

He breathed out onto the mirror but no condensation crystallized. He touched his chest, feeling for his heartbeat but the cold cube within wasn't beating. Of course he still didn't know what was wrong with him and may have stayed that way for quite a while if not for the door to his bedroom opening. In marched his small entourage of a half dozen of his minions. Each was carrying a piece of his breakfast, whether it was a glass of juice or a dish of food, while another brought his cloths and another the newspaper of a town in the north he enjoyed reading about. Whenever he made it snow—the town, which was a ski resort—praised him to no end.

"Ah, it's time for breakfast," he said as the minions set up a table at the far end of the room and laid out the food, newspaper, and other items. But as he sat down, Snow Miser realized he was hungry, but not for the food on the table. His eyes went to the closest minion, and as he studied the little fella's small neck, he felt his stomach rumble with a craving he'd never had before.

Before any of his entourage knew what was happening, Snow Miser lunged for the closest one, grabbed him, and pulled the little guy to his mouth, taking a good-sized chunk of cold flesh from his neck.

Blood squirted out of the gaping neck wound to freeze as it hit the floor. Snow Miser dropped the little version of himself to the floor as he chewed happily. The rest of the group stared in shock at their brother, not quite understanding what was happening.

Snow Miser stood up, crossed the room and slammed the bedroom door closed.

"That was just a light snack, boys, now it's time for the real meal," he laughed.

The group of mini-versions of Snow Miser all swallowed as one, as they stared up at their master.

Then Snow Miser ran at the next one in line, his teeth shredding flesh, his hands tearing at tiny skin.

The killing began in earnest.

Santa was dreaming.

He was in the stable back at the North Pole and for some reason he had fallen down and was lying on the hay-covered ground. A reindeer was on his chest and it was sniffing him. He could feel its breath on his face and hear the huffing of its rasping lungs as each intake of air was exhaled. Only the breath wasn't warm, it was cold—ice cold.

He crinkled his nose at the odor of feces and the smell of bad meat. It reminded him of the time Martha had left thawing meat in the back of the refrigerator for far too long after forgetting about it.

The meat had become rancid, turning green. That was the odor that tickled his nostrils now.

Suddenly, the dream wasn't a dream but was real as he felt something nibble the tip of his nose. But before whatever had a grip on him could do more than press on his nose, his eyes snapped open and he found himself looking into the dead eyes of Vixen.

The reindeer was on his chest, her teeth clamped on his nose, and from the pressure Santa felt, she was about to snap her jaws closed and take his nose clean off. Acting fast, he shoved his hands between her upper and lower jaws and spread his arms apart, separating her teeth from his nose. It wasn't easy, because he was lying down and had no leverage, but he only needed to move her teeth a fraction of an inch. As he did it, the move was enough and his nose was free a moment later. Santa turned his face away as he pulled his hands out of her mouth, her teeth snapping closed with a loud *clacking* sound.

"Vixen, what in blazes is wrong with you!" Santa yelled and sat up, pushing the reindeer off him. Vixen fell off Santa and rolled to the foot of the bed, but then jumped up to face him. Her rear haunches were pointed up, her head low to the bed, her teeth showing as she growled from deep within her throat. Her eyes creased and Santa knew she was going to attack him.

Simultaneously, as Vixen jumped at Santa's face again, Santa reached around and grabbed his pillow, swinging it around to use as a shield. Vixen's teeth sank into the pillow and began to tear at it, fluffy feathers filling the air to rain down on the floor like snow.

Santa fought with the small reindeer, in shock at the viciousness and strength the small doe was showing. He wondered if it was due to her being sick, as he fought to keep her at bay. She was nothing but snapping teeth and raking hooves.

Santa managed to get off the bed, and as Vixen swung her head wildly to the side to toss away the deflated pillow in her mouth, Santa reached for the blanket on the bed and threw it over Vixen just before she tried to charge him again. Wrapped in the blanket, the doe began to hiss and growl. Santa moved in fast, grabbing the ends of the blanket and pulling them together so that all four corners were in his hands. Then taking the empty pillow in one of his hands while the other held onto the corners of the blanket, he used the torn material like a rope and tied the ends of the blanket so that he had a makeshift sack. Within the blanket, Vixen howled and growled as she tried to get free.

Santa took a step back and stared at the sack on the bed containing the once gentle reindeer. Within the blanket, Vixen gnashed her teeth as she tried to escape her cloth prison.

Seeing that the reindeer was trapped for the moment, Santa quickly dressed, and with a slam of the bedroom door, left the room. He needed to find Martha, and fast.

Mrs. Claus was pulled from sleep by what she thought were elves pounding on wood as they made toys for Christmas. But as she slowly opened her eyes, she realized someone was at her door.

Getting out of bed, she padded across the floor of ice and opened the door…and promptly fell back when Santa Claus came barreling in, slamming the door after he was inside.

"Maw, it's terrible. Something's happened to Vixen. She tried to attack me, bite me even."

Mrs. Claus was still groggy from sleep and she blinked at her long-time husband, while trying to wake up and take in what he was saying. "What are you talking about, dear?" she asked as she went back to her bed and sat on the edge. The room was cold and she wanted to get back into her warm and snugly ice bed, in which the magic was working correctly and had kept her quite comfortable while she slept.

Santa told the story about Vixen, and when he finished, he stared at his wife, who was looking at him as if he was crazy.

"Well, don't just sit there, Maw, we need to do something? Vixen's gone crazy!"

There was a knock on the door and Mrs. Claus looked to Santa and then the door. "Oh my, it's Grand Central Station in here." She got up and went to the door, opening it to see Jingle and Jangle looking up at her, both with bleary eyes.

"Mrs. C, are you all right?" Jingle asked.

"Yeah," Jangle added. "We were both woken up when we heard yelling coming from your room."

"Oh, Jingle, Jangle, it's good you're here. Come inside. Santa has told me something awful." The elves quickly shuffled into the room. "Okay, dear," Mrs. Claus said to Santa once the elves were inside. "Tell me one more time with the boys here."

Santa did as he was told, his arms waving in the air before him as he became animated, reliving the experience one more time. When he was through, he felt exhausted and sat on the edge of the bed to rest.

"Oh no, Vixen sounds like she's really sick," Jingle said to Mrs. Claus. "What do we do, Mrs. C?"

"Well, dear," she said to Jingle as she considered Santa's story. "We need to get her back to the North Pole where Dr. Crackle can have a look at her." Crackle was the North Pole veterinarian and he took care of all the reindeer. "But first we should go see Snow Miser and tell him what's happening. Maybe he can do something to help."

Santa was so frazzled that he didn't even flinch at the mention of Snow Miser's name. If the cold blowhard could help, Santa was all for it and he said as much. "That's a good idea, Maw, let's go see him. Maybe he can do something to help the poor little girl."

"Just let me get dressed and then we'll go," Mrs. Claus said. "I won't be but a minute." She gathered her clothes and went into the bathroom, returning a few minutes later, dressed. "There, all set. I'm sure Snowy will be able to help us," she said with confidence as the group of four filed out of the bedroom. "I mean, he may be a big ham, but he is the Snow Miser after all."

The Grand Hall where Snow Miser received his guests was empty when Santa and the others arrived. Like the rest of Snow Miser's castle, the large room was made of ice, including the throne located in the middle of the room.

Santa was about to ask Mrs. Claus what she thought they should do next when a door at the far end of the room slammed open and Snow Miser appeared in the doorway.

Only he didn't look the way Santa had seen him the day before. While always pale, now Snow Miser was even whiter. His eyes had sunk into his head, the face gaunt and hollow. Cracks in the frozen skin could be seen and some of his ice-hair had fallen out.

But that was nothing compared to his state of attire. His clothing was covered in what looked like frozen ketchup, but as Snow Miser walked closer, Santa saw he was carrying something in his right hand, and was chewing on it as if it was a turkey leg.

When Snow Miser was only ten feet away, Santa's eyes went wide upon the realization that Snow Miser was gnawing on a small arm—the same size as one of his little minions.

"Ah, fatso, and the elves, and Mrs. C, all here in one place," Snow Miser said. "Excellent. This saves time so I don't have to chase all of you down in your rooms."

"You don't look too well," Santa said. "What's wrong with you? And why in the blazes are you eating an arm?"

Snow Miser smiled, his blood-stained teeth showing through his thin lips. "Ah, and there's the rub, fatso," he said. "It seems something has happened to me since last night." He held up his arm to show off his wounded wrist to Santa and the others. "I think this is the culprit. Your reindeer is sick and whatever it has, it's given it to me when it bit me. But that's okay, because you know why? I like what I've become." He turned his head and called out to his minions. "Come on in, boys, show the Clauses your new look." More than two dozen minions entered the Grand Hall, but they were all zombies now, the scalps on their heads sitting there like top hats, frozen blood seeping from under their pale pates. Their throats had all been torn out, more frozen blood on their small suits, their attire matching Zombie Miser perfectly.

They gathered around Snow Miser, a deep hunger in their dead eyes as they eyed the group of four, licking their lips at the warm flesh standing only a few feet before them.

"Snowy," Mrs. Claus said. "What's the meaning of this? We need your help."

Snow Miser laughed. "Ah, my sweet little icicle, I think I shall save you for last. But please, don't call me Snowy or even Snow Miser anymore. For you see, since last night, I've taken on a new title."

"And that is?" Santa asked.

"Call me Zombie Miser," he said and turned to his minions, while yelling out, "Hit it, boys!"

Music began to play from hidden speakers as Zombie Miser began to dance, his minions all right beside him.

[Zombie Miser]
I'm Mr. Zombie Miser,

I'm Mister Death.
I'm Mister Walking Corpse,
I am Mister No Breath.
People call me Zombie Miser!
Whatever I bite,
Begins to rot in my mouth!
I'm too dead!

[Chorus—Minions: The little Zombie Misers. While dancing, they would take off the top of their skulls as if they were hats.]
He's Mister Zombie Miser.
He's Mister Death.

[Zombie Miser]
Yes I am!

[Chorus—Minions]
He's Mister Walking Corpse,
He is Mister No Breath!

[Zombie Miser]
People call me Zombie Miser
Whatever I bite,
Begins to rot in my mouth!
I'm too dead!

[Chorus—Minions]
He's too dead!

[Zombie Miser]
I never want to see a day.
That's not filled with dying folk.

I'd rather have 'em dead and rotting,
One, two, three, a million!

[Chorus—Minions]
He's Mister Zombie Miser,
He's Mister Death.

[Snow Miser]
That's me!

[Chorus]
He's Mister Zombie Miser,
He is Mister No Breath!

[Zombie Miser]
People call me Zombie Miser
Whatever I bite,
Begins to rot in my mouth!
…too dead!

[Minions]
Too dead!

"Huh, that's catchy," Santa said. "Tell me, is that part of being a zombie? Breaking out into song for no justifiable reason?"

"Hey, fatso, I'm a Miser. I can do whatever I want. If I want to take off all my clothes and run around naked, I can."

"Oh, please don't do that, this is a family show after all," Mrs. Claus said and winced, the image of a naked and skinny Miser haunting her mind.

"So, Zombie Miser, if that's your name now. Why the dance number?" Santa asked.

Zombie Miser shrugged. "Oh, it was just to lull you all into a false sense of security." He looked at his minions. "Go 'head, boys, get 'em. It's time for breakfast."

As one, the minions hissed and moaned, then charged Santa and his wife, as well as Jingle and Jangle, the hunger in their eyes apparent to all who stood with mouths hanging agape in horror.

Santa looked at his wife and sighed. "I swear, Maw, I should have just stayed in bed back at the North Pole." Then he raised his hands, curled them into fists, and prepared for a battle with the undead minions.

At first, Jingle and Jangle cowered behind Mrs. Claus, but when she yelled at them to fight or else they would all die, the two elves gathered what courage they could find and joined the battle.

Mrs. Claus hadn't said much since arriving in the Grand Hall but there was no need. What she was seeing with her eyes was enough for her to accept it as real. And after taking into account what Santa had told her about Vixen...well, she wasn't a stupid woman and never wasted time arguing what her own eyes told her. Besides, she lived in a world where magic was common. If a fat man in a red suit could deliver Christmas presents to the entire world in one night by using flying reindeer that towed a large, red, open sleigh, then zombies didn't seem that farfetched.

She retreated a few feet and picked up an ice chair, then smashed it onto the ice floor. The chair shattered into a dozen pieces and she grabbed a broken leg. The ice was cold in her hand but the leg was now nothing but a giant icicle with a sharp tip. She shoved it out in front of her as the minions charged, yelling at Jingle and Jangle to get pieces of the chair as well to use as weapons.

Santa went for a different tactic.

After four minions ran at him, Santa punched and kicked them away. The little people rolled across the floor like bowling balls only to get up at the end of their travel, turn, and race back at Santa to continue the fight.

Santa Claus spotted an old sack lying in a corner of the room and he spun around on his heels and dashed for it, the four zombie minions following close behind. Off to the side, Zombie Miser laughed and clapped as he danced a jig.

Santa ran right into the wall as he slid on the ice floor, then scooped up the sack and held it before him with a smile. "Now, it's my turn," he said with a sparkle in his eye.

Every Christmas, Santa used magic to get all the presents to each home of good little boys and girls. He did this by having a bottomless sack of toys. Now, though he used a large red sack with embroidery on it, in reality, any old sack would do. Even a lunch bag would work in a pinch, though he could only take out toys as big as the sack opening. The sack in his hands now had a good-sized opening, and with a wave of his free hand, he plunged it into the sack and began fishing around, while the other hand held the sack by its opening.

Just as the minions reached him, Santa pulled out a hockey stick, and with a laugh that made his belly shake like a bowl full of jelly, he began whacking at the minions, taking off heads and legs with each blow.

As soon as he finished off his tiny attackers, he reached into the sack and began rummaging for more goodies. Pulling out a handful of candy canes, he yelled to Jingle and Jangle and threw the candy canes at the two elves. "Use them like daggers!" he instructed.

Jingle caught three of them and Jangle caught two, the elves spinning the candy canes around so that the hooks were pointed at them, then they began stabbing at the zombie minions with the bottom tips as the minions tried to bite the elves.

Jangle closed his eyes and lunged forward with a candy cane as if it was a sword. Though quite by accident, his aim was true and the tip of the candy cane slid into the left eye of a minion as the little zombie charged at the elf. Jangle cringed as he felt the tip of the candy cane slide into the eye socket, grating on bone as a pinkish fluid oozed out around the candy cane. When Jangle withdrew the weapon, the minion's eyeball was still stuck to the tip, the impaled orb looking like a mushroom on a kebab stick. But the candy cane had penetrated into the brain as well and the zombie minion dropped to the floor, dead for good.

Jangle turned and promptly threw up all over his red outfit.

Mrs. Claus was an Amazon woman in all but attire. She swung the icicle she'd taken from the broken chair back and forth, taking down minions one at a time. She plunged the icicle into the chest of the closest small zombie, the tip bursting out of the little guy's back, covered in red. But the minion still clawed at Mrs. Claus, sliding its body down the icicle so it could get at her. Using her foot, she kicked it off and then stabbed downward into its head, killing it when the icicle impaled the brain.

Heaving heavily, she spun around to see who was in need of dying next.

Santa had pulled out some ornaments and he threw them onto the floor, where the minions stepped on them, crushing them beneath their feet. The sharp shards impaled their slipper-like footwear and the flesh within but the minions felt no pain and just kept coming. Frowning when that didn't work, Santa reached into the sack and pulled out a BB gun. Cocking the weapon, he began firing at the zombie minions' faces, more than one BB penetrating an eye and the brain behind it, taking out the small zombies before they knew what was happening.

Jingle punched and kicked his attackers, using the candy cane he held as a dagger, just like Santa had told him. He plunged the tip again and again into minions until their chest cavities were gaping open, their insides dripping out to splash onto the frozen floor. Then Jingle would finally deal the killing blow, stabbing the candy cane in either an eye or an ear hole. One time, when the angle was bad, he jammed the candy cane up a minion's nose, sliding it into the nasal canal, then he twisted and felt the weapon slip into the brain cavity. When the small body went limp, Jingle knew he'd hit paydirt.

The battle was furious, Santa and Mrs. Claus stomping on bodies and snapping necks to sever spinal cords, a pile of small bodies surrounding them.

Santa pulled out firecrackers, set them alight, and jammed them into open mouths when the minions tried to snap at him with their teeth. Exploding, the firecrackers were like small grenades, blowing off heads and leaving tottering, headless bodies that would sometimes keep walking before finally falling over.

And then the battle was over, only Zombie Miser remaining.

"You haven't won anything, fatso!" Zombie Miser screamed from the far end of the room as he prepared to make his escape through a back door. "As long as I'm alive, I can infect anyone I please. In a matter of hours, I can have an army of undead at my disposal!"

"Well, we can't have that now, can we," Santa said and reached into the sack and pulled out a genuine tomahawk, the edge of the axe head razor sharp. Dropping the sack, Santa weighed the tomahawk in his hand to get the feel of it, then with the expertise only magic could deliver, he pulled back his arm and threw the tomahawk at Zombie Miser. The steel weapon zipped through the air, the light dancing off the polished metal sheen.

Zombie Miser was just turning to flee when the tomahawk struck him on the back of the head. The axe end of the weapon embedded itself into his skull with a meaty thwack, practically splitting his face in half. He slumped to the floor, gray brain matter seeping out of the jagged wound to freeze as it touched the floor of ice.

"Well, I'll be," Mrs. Claus said, impressed, her hands on her hips. "I didn't know you could do that."

Santa shrugged. "Maw, there's a lot you don't know about me. Even after all these years I still have a few tricks up my sleeve." He gave her a wink and she smiled.

"Can we please leave here now, Mrs. C," Jingle asked as he stood in a pile of gore. Jangle nodded, too, wanting to leave this charnel house behind him.

"That is an excellent idea, boys," she said. "Let's get to Dasher and Blitzen and fly away from here. There's four of us, Santa and I can ride a reindeer each with one of you boys on each of our laps."

She went to Santa and kissed him on the cheek, ignoring the frozen blood splatter there. they were all covered in blood and gore. With one last look at the carnage, she and Santa turned and walked out of the Grand Hall, the two elves following close behind.

"I tell you, Santa," Mrs. Claus said as they were leaving. "I'm not looking forward to explaining all this to Snow Miser's brother Heat Miser."

"One issue at a time, Maw, one issue at a time," Santa said as they walked down the hallway that led to the stable, where the two reindeer were being kept.

Soon, the group of four was flying to the North Pole, with Santa on Blitzen and Mrs. Claus on Dasher, an elf perched on each of their laps.

"So, dear," Mrs. Claus said to Santa. "Are you going out this Christmas Eve to deliver presents?"

"Yes I am," Santa replied. "After what we've been through, I've shaken off my melancholy."

"Good, then at last something good has come from this terrible experience," she said as they flew off into the horizon.

Back at Zombie Miser's ice castle, all was quiet, the zombies destroyed for good.

But as time went by, there came a sound. It was faint but slowly grew louder.

In the bedroom Santa Claus had slept in, Vixen finally managed to chew through the blanket keeping her prisoner. In his haste to leave, Santa had forgotten about Vixen.

Once free of the blanket, her head snapped back and forth as she looked for Santa, but seeing that the room was empty, she began to look for a way out. That came soon enough when her eyes fell upon the only window in the room.

Without pause, she leapt off the bed and through the window, glass crashing around her. One jagged shard of glass embedded itself in her front leg, but she ignored it, feeling no pain.

Though a zombie, she still had the power of flight, and she turned and flew away from the castle, back down to earth, which was only now awakening from a long night.

As she flew over Southtown, USA, she could see people already about, some going for a morning walk, some getting the newspaper, while others were on their way to work.

Picking a target, she soared down and attacked a hapless man, her teeth sinking into warm flesh before the man knew what was happening. As soon as she finished chewing on the man, a woman appeared from around the corner at the end of the street. Leaping into the air, Vixen flew at the woman, taking her down to the ground by running into her chest. Standing on the woman, Vixen's head snapped down and she tore out the woman's throat. Chewing happily, her eyes lit on another pedestrian and soon she was feeding on that unlucky soul.

And so it began, as each time Vixen took down a victim, said victim rose from the dead to join in the slaughter. By the end of the day, Southtown would be a home for the living dead, and the remaining humans would be cowering for their lives and then it would spread across the globe.

It's wasn't over yet. In fact, it was only the beginning… of an undead Christmas.

NO MORE CHRISTMAS

Mike Reynolds stared at his two daughters as they played by the fireplace. Watching the two children, and becoming lost in their imagination as they played with their old toys, he found he could pretend the dead never walked and that the world wasn't an apocalyptic cesspool, filled with rotting corpses and the animated dead.

The calendar on the wall, the one with all the blocks crossed out, said that tomorrow was December 24th.

It would be Christmas in two days and Mike had decided that no matter what, it would be a Christmas his two daughters would remember.

He had decided to leave their small cabin in the woods, about twenty miles from the closest city, and go into the nearest town and scavenge what presents he could find for his family.

Over the past year, their morale had waned and he knew this would be just the thing to raise the children's spirits. Of course, his wife, Sharon, didn't want him to go and had vehemently argued for him to stay.

"But don't you see, honey," Mike had told her the previous night. "The girls need something to remind them of what life was like before the dead walked. They need to feel like the world could be the way it was again."

"But it's too dangerous , you know that," she had said as the two whispered by the fresh-cut Christmas tree Mike had brought into the cabin three days earlier. It was decorated with whatever odds and ends they could find in the cabin, as well as small twigs that had been tied together to mimic garland. The top of the tree had a small wooden carving of an angel. It wasn't a very good likeness, but it was the best Mike could do given his skill level.

"What if you get cornered somewhere?" she asked. "What if you're trapped or hurt? We'll never know what happened to you. What kind of Christmas would it be for the girls then, for me? What if their father never came home?"

Mike had waved away her concerns with his hand. "I've made my mind up, Sharon, I'm doing this. Our girls need to have a real Christmas again, even if it's only for one day, they need to be happy."

Tears welled up in Sharon's eyes as she hugged her husband. "You just better come back to us, you hear?" she sniffed. "You better not leave us alone."

He patted her back softly, then rubbed it in small circles and began caressing her neck. After a full minute had elapsed, he disengaged himself from her and held her shoulders with his hands.

"Sharon, you should know by now that nothing would ever keep me away from you and the girls. Why, death itself wouldn't stop me."

She sniffed a little more and regained her composure, feeling slightly embarrassed by her show of emotion. She knew Mike didn't need her crying like a weak woman and have her welfare on his mind. No, if he was really going out into the world, even if it was against her wishes, she would support him with everything she had.

"I still don't like this, but I have to admit, even though I don't want you to go, it would be nice for the girls to have presents to open on Christmas morning. You just better keep your promise and get back here in one piece."

"I'll be fine," he told her with as much confidence as he could muster. "You'll see; I'll be back before you even know I'm gone."

The next morning found Mike leaving his car and walking the last half mile to the town.

It had been a hard morning for him.

After hugging his daughters and telling them goodbye, Sharon had reconsidered, and begged him to stay with them.

But his mind was made up and he had left her in tears, the girls not understanding why Mommy was crying. She had been on her knees, hugging the two girls as he drove away. He had glanced in the rearview mirror one last time before taking a bend in the dirt road, the cabin quickly lost from sight.

The cabin had been his father's, and when the dead began to walk, Mike knew it was the only safe place to be—in the middle of nowhere, where the dead couldn't get them.

Still, every now and then a zombie would find the old dirt road leading to the cabin and Mike would have to put the thing down, using the machete to hack it to pieces like it was cordwood. There was an open pit a hundred feet from the cabin where he dumped the bodies and parts. It was already half full. Soon, he would have to cover it and make another. But he'd worry about that when the time came.

As he walked into town, he glanced one last time at the car, making sure it was well concealed.

It wasn't perfectly hidden, but it should be fine for the half day he figured he'd be gone. Then, with gifts in hand, he would return to his family and they would all celebrate a wonderful Christmas together.

He hoped to find some canned goods as well, maybe even some sweet potatoes and canned ham. That would make Christmas even better.

In his pocket he had a list of some likely presents. For the girls he was looking for dolls—any kind would do—as well as coloring books and crayons. For Sharon, perfume and any makeup he could find, as well as new pants and shirts. Out of the four of them, Sharon had the littlest amount of clothing and had to wear the same things over and over. Mike knew she would be thrilled to get a new outfit for Christmas.

For weapons, he carried his trusty machete for quiet work and had a hunting rifle slung over his shoulder by a strap. The gun was only for emergencies, as its report would alert the dead for miles that he was in the vicinity, and if that happened, it wouldn't be very good for his plan of going into town unobserved.

He walked slowly through the woods, cutting through the forest instead of following the road into town. He hoped by doing this he could sneak in quietly and unnoticed. He knew there had been rioting after the dead began to walk and frankly, he had no idea what to expect in the town.

Whether danger came from the undead or from fellow living survivors, he didn't know and he didn't want to know. If he had his wish, he would get in, search some homes for possible gifts, then get back out without a soul—living or dead—ever seeing him.

At the outskirts of the town, he paused and just stood motionless for five minutes. He strained to hear anything that would mark the presence of danger. When nothing came to pass, he continued on, stepping out of the treeline and onto the road leading into the north side of town.

It was a small town, no more than three thousand people in total, but how many were living there now was anyone's guess.

Mike assumed the entire town was evacuated when Martial Law had gone into effect, but he wouldn't know for sure until he went into some of the homes.

The first house was only a few minutes walk from the treeline and he approached it cautiously.

The front of the home was decorated with Christmas decorations. A plastic snowman was on the yellow, overgrown lawn and a sleigh with a smiling Santa waving—also made of plastic—sat on the roof, the extension cord for the electricity still dangling from where it had popped off its moorings. Large bulbs of red, yellow and blue adorned the window frames, but all were dark as the power had long failed in this part of the state.

As he crossed the street and onto the front lawn, he paused when he saw a lone figure at the end of the street. It was walking slowly and seemed to pause and look at him. But then it continued on, to be lost behind another building. Mike knew then it had to be one of the walking dead, for a living person wouldn't have continued on like that.

Unknown to Mike, the animated corpse had seen him, but from a distance, the zombie assumed Mike was just another animated corpse and had ignored him.

Mike continued on to the stone walkway and up to the porch of the home.

He barely glanced at the dry and brown wreath on the front door, now a year old.

Not knowing what to expect, he reached out and tried the doorknob.

Turning it slowly, he was only mildly surprised when the door clicked open on greased hinges. As he stepped in slowly, the machete in his right hand, he sniffed deeply for signs of the dead. Their odor was unmistakable, like rotting trash left out in the sun for too long.

Though the house smelled of stale air, he didn't detect the ripeness of the walking dead and he entered with a little more confidence. As he stepped inside, closing the door softly, he looked down to see the skeleton of a housecat. The animal must have been left behind at the evacuation and had starved to death when food had run out. Stepping over the small skeleton with bits of dry skin and fur, he headed deeper into the home, his destination the living room.

Just as he expected, the room was decorated with Christmas cheer. A once fresh tree—now brown, the needles on the floor around it like a carpet—was in the far corner and under the tree, also covered with brown needles, were faded presents, each wrapped and waiting for a recipient that would never be.

But before Mike could inspect the presents, a door at the back of the house banged open and three zombies stumbled into the living room, moaning in that dry rasping voice Mike knew so well. As they approached, their stench hit him and he fought the urge to gag as bile crept up into his throat.

His first urge was to sling his rifle off his shoulder and shoot them, but he knew it would be a mistake. Even inside the house, the report of the rifle would alert others to his location, especially when the town was as quiet as a grave. Sound carried far and the rifle shot would be like an explosion in the abandoned town.

No, this was a job for the machete, and with it still in his right hand, he raised it over his head and prepared for battle.

The first zombie to come at him was an old man, looking at least eighty, but due to the withered skin and pale complexion of death, it was hard to tell precisely. Not that it mattered. Even the geriatric dead had a new spring to their step upon reanimating. Perhaps it was that the dead felt no pain, so ailments such as arthritis and cataracts didn't bother them any more.

Mike waited for the old man to get within three feet of him and he sliced sideways with the machete. The blade was razor sharp and it took off the old man's head as if it was made of dry paper.

The head tumbled off the body's shoulders to fall before it, and the shuffling feet kicked it aside before the corpse dropped to the floor, a black ooze seeping out of the jagged neck stump.

The other two zombies barely slowed their gait, but now had to step over or around the now headless corpse. Mike used this hesitation to his advantage and swung the machete like an axe, slicing off the next zombie's hands at the wrists. The ghoul floundered as black blood seeped from the wounds, and as it reached for Mike, not understanding why it couldn't grab him, Mike finished it off with a chop to the head, slicing the dry skull in two. Like a cut melon, both sides spilled over to flop onto each shoulder, more black ooze spilling forth.

The last zombie had been a woman, and still was to Mike. Wearing a red Christmas sweater with withered mistletoe pinned to her chest, even in death Mike could see she had been a beautiful woman. Her blonde hair was plastered to her head, the roots pulled out and bloody in many spots. One of her eyes was missing, and Mike imagined the remaining one had once been a deep blue to match her blonde hair.

She opened her mouth and elicited a dry moan, rasping, like the voice of a heavy smoker. It almost seemed to him that she was trying to…talk.

He hesitated giving her the killing blow and it was almost his downfall. As he stared at her, she suddenly lunged for him, stepping onto the corpse of the old man and then seeming to jump into the air. Before Mike realized what was happening, he was being forced back into the withered Christmas tree, the dead woman on top of him.

In a crash of pine needles and dry branches, they tumbled to the floor amidst the faded presents.

Mike lost his machete in the fall and his rifle became trapped underneath him. All the while, the zombie was trying to snap at him, her once pristine teeth now cracked and yellow.

He reached out for something to use as a weapon with his left hand as his right held the zombie at bay. His fingers wrapped around a present and he tore it open, the chore harder for the lack of two hands. As he tore open the box, he grabbed what was within it and brought it up to use as a weapon. But when he saw it was a video game controller, he realized he had come up empty.

With nothing else to use, he slammed it into the dead woman's nose, the hard plastic smashing it flat. Dry air wheezed forth as yellow mucus dripped out of the open cavity. He used the controller again, slamming it into her forehead, and a soft crack came to him. Still, she renewed her attack, teeth clacking on empty air. Desperate and out of options, he jammed the controller into her mouth, breaking teeth off as the hard plastic slid into her gullet.

He jammed it in there so good it was like a large ball gag, and try as she might, she couldn't get it out.

With her teeth no longer a danger, Mike reached up with his left hand and grabbed her head, then shifted his right to the other side, and with a mighty twist, he snapped her neck, the loud crack filling the house like a cannon had gone off.

The zombie's arms and legs stopped moving as the connection from brain to body became severed, but still the remaining eye blinked. The brain was still active.

But Mike knew the ghoul was harmless now and he pushed it off him with a groan. He stumbled to his feet and retrieved his machete, then with one last look at the three destroyed zombies, decided he didn't want to stay in the house a moment longer.

After gathering a few presents up in his arms, he left, relishing the fresh air as he stepped outside. He checked the street and it was clear for the moment—nothing in sight—either living or dead.

Sitting on the porch, he began opening the presents, hoping to find something he could use.

He ripped into the first one and frowned when he saw what it was.

An electric razor with a charger.

With no power, it was useless. He tossed it aside.

The second one was no better. A handheld video game system. But it needed batteries and he had run out of batteries six months ago. He tossed it onto the overgrown lawn where it disappeared in the weeds.

The third present was actually something he could use. It was a brand new Stanley claw hammer. He slid it through a loop on his pants for safekeeping. It worked well as a weapon and as a tool, and the one he had at the cabin was more than twenty years old with a wooden handle. The Stanley was all solid metal.

There was one last present and he opened it quickly. As the wrapping paper fell to the ground to blow away, he saw there was another, smaller box within the first one. Opening this one, he found a pair of diamond earrings.

Though items such as gold and diamonds were a thing of the past, he still pocketed them. He would give them to Sharon. He knew she would like them, even if it was frivolous.

As he watched the wrapping paper blow across the street and get stuck in some bushes, he sighed heavily.

Well, what did he expect? That he would enter the first house and come out with all he wanted? Of course not.

Standing, he brushed off the stray bits of paper and tape, and headed down the street, to try another house.

Christmas decorations adorned telephone poles, most now weathered and torn. A plastic reindeer lay in the middle of the road where it had blown out of a yard after a storm months ago.

The face was pitted and the paint scratched and faded, and dried blood covered the back of it.

Mike walked around it, barely seeing it. All around him was wreckage. Abandoned cars with their doors hanging open—animals such as raccoons and skunks now using the cars as homes—were everywhere, and many homes showed signs of fire damage. Gutters on the houses were overgrown with dirt, and weeds grew out of them as if they were long window boxes, the vines hanging down.

Kudzu had returned in force, filling once manicured lawns to almost waist high, as well as growing between shrubs and bushes once trimmed and now runaway messes.

As Mike turned a corner, he spotted another lone figure standing in the middle of the road, about fifty feet away. The instant he saw the figure, the figure saw him also, and it began shambling toward him.

As it moved closer, Mike saw it was a man in a Santa Claus suit, only this suit was covered in dried blood and pus. When Santa was close enough for Mike to see the man's face, he saw it wasn't a man but yet one more zombie.

The white beard was gone and Santa's lower jaw was missing. The tongue hung down like a short necktie, the black muscle twitching back and forth. A low, gurgle of a moan escaped Santa as he began to hobble faster toward Mike.

Gritting his teeth at this display of holiday death, Mike raised his machete and prepared to put Santa down for good.

Each figure moved toward the other, and when Mike was close enough, he raised the machete high and brought it down, planning on slicing Santa's head in half. But at the last second, by accident or intent, Santa moved to the side and the machete came down on his shoulder. The blade sank six inches into dead flesh and became jammed between bone. When Mike tried to pull the blade free, he found it was stuck.

Santa barely flinched as his body was impaled by steel, and he reached out with unusually large hands and wrapped them around Mike's throat. As Mike tried to escape, he and Santa fell to the road to begin fighting.

Once more, Mike's rifle was jammed under his body and he cursed his luck.

Santa's tongue draped over his face, only an inch from Mike's nose as he struggled to keep the zombie at bay. Meanwhile, the holiday zombie was squeezing the life out of Mike's throat and he was beginning to lose focus as lack of oxygen threatened to cause him to faint.

Once more, he reached down to his side, desperate to find a weapon, and his hand found the Stanley hammer.

Pulling it free of his pants with a ripping of material, he spun it around so the claw was facing Santa. With a meaty thwack, he brought the hammer down, the claw embedding itself two inches into Santa's skull.

The zombie seemed to grunt as the hammer slammed into his head, but then he continued to try and bite Mike, despite the lack of a lower jaw. With a tearing of rotting flesh and bone, Mike pulled the hammer free and brought it down again. This time the claw went in deeper and managed to hit brain matter. Santa jerked like he was being electrocuted, and his white eyes rolled up into the back of his head as he slumped forward, limp, his hands releasing their death grip on Mike's throat.

Mike didn't move at first, just glad to be alive. Then with a heave, he rolled Santa off him. He rolled a few feet away and lay on the road, panting. His face was covered in slobber and he felt like he was going to vomit at any moment. Small pinpricks of light still danced across his vision and his throat felt raw when he tried to swallow.

Sitting up, he waited for the nausea to pass and then went to his feet. He pulled the machete from the corpse, and after wiping the blade on the back of Santa's red suit, he did the same with the claw hammer.

Now, with tools clean, he hobbled away, looking for all purposes like a zombie himself.

He walked another half block before he decided he needed to go someplace and rest for a bit. There was a house on his right that had all its doors closed and windows were intact, so with hopes of a sterile environment inside, one devoid of the dead, he limped to the front door.

It was locked but the hammer took care of that, a few whacks to the doorknob breaking it off. Then, with a good kick, the door flew in.

Mike waited for more than two full minutes, to see if anything or anyone would come out of the shadows and attack him, and when nothing did, he headed inside.

He planned on finding a couch or a bed and rest for at least an hour, then he would continue his search.

He made sure to close the door and prop a chair under it. There was a one foot tall crystal statue of an angel on a side table, and he placed it on the chair. If something tried to get in, the statue would fall and shatter, alerting him of trouble.

Barely looking at the house itself, he stumbled into the living room. The couch was there, as it was in every home he'd ever been in, and he fell onto it with a weary sigh. As he closed his eyes, he never even knew when he drifted off into an exhausted, stress-filled sleep.

Mike snapped awake with a jerk and an intake of breath. Then he winced, the breathing painful thanks to the soreness of his throat. Damn Santa zombie had almost killed him.

As he looked around the living room, he was relieved to see it was the same as when he fell asleep. The house smelled stale but not of death, and it was as empty as when he arrived.

His eyes caught a small birdcage in the corner, hanging from a metal post. Standing on weak legs, he shuffled over to it.

In the bottom of the cage was the dried husk of a canary, the date on the newspaper on the floor of the cage only three days before the world fell apart.

He could read the headline when he cocked his head a little. **IS IT A HOAX? DO THE DEAD REALLY WALK? SCIENTIST BAFFLED!** In smaller font, *Christmas shopping at an all time low due to crisis!*

Scratching his head, he felt his bladder alerting him it needed to be emptied. Wandering down the first hallway he spotted, he quickly found the bathroom. He peed in the toilet and even flushed it. But as the water went down, there was none to refill the tank. The water pressure had failed more than six months ago if not more, depending on the area.

He checked the medicine chest and found two bottles of aspirin and an open box of sleeping pills. He put them all in his pocket. A half empty tube of toothpaste sat on the end of the sink and he took that, too. Then he headed back into the living room to inspect the presents. He had already decided after this house he would head back home.

He'd already managed to burn through half a day and he knew he wanted to be home before nightfall. Being December, it was dark by four in the afternoon, and he knew he wouldn't want to be out once the sun went down.

Sitting cross-legged by the withered tree, for all purposes looking like a boy on Christmas morning, Mike reached out and picked up a present. Beside him sat his machete, rifle and hammer.

The box was heavy and for a moment it felt like something was alive inside it, but of course that would be ridiculous. The present had sat under the tree for an entire year, nothing could be alive inside.

He quickly tore off the paper, and as he pulled open the flaps of the box, he was horrified to find more than two dozen mice inside. As he stared at the little creatures, they swarmed out of the box and onto his arms, then onto his shirt. Cringing in horror, despite knowing the mice were harmless, he dropped the box and jumped up, brushing the rodents off him. They fell to the floor and scurried under the couch, chairs, and anywhere else they could find. As he regained control of himself, he looked down into the box and saw two things at the same time. The first was the wrapper of a fruitcake, now empty and chewed up from tiny teeth. The second was the hole on the back of the present, where the mice had burrowed in and fed on the sweet treat and then made the box their nest.

As the tail of the last mouse disappeared under a chair, Mike shook himself and reached for another present. This time he held it steady and gave it a gentle shake. When nothing moved within, he tore it open and peered inside. It was an iPod. Disgusted at finding another worthless present, he tossed it aside and tried another. This time he had some luck. It was a cashmere sweater. He set it aside to bring home to Sharon.

He went through the other presents and ended up with a pile of junk off to his left. A year ago, the items would have been worth a small fortune, but in the world of the walking dead, they were worth less than rocks. At least rocks could be used as throwing weapons in a pinch.

Standing up, he decided to search the rest of the house before leaving. He didn't like the idea of leaving empty handed and of returning to the cabin the same way. The girls were counting on him as he had told them he was going hunting for Christmas presents.

Leaving the living room with his machete in his hand and the rifle and hammer back on his person, he walked past the bathroom to search the rest of the house. The first bedroom he came to belonged to the adults of the home, and when he peered inside, he frowned at the sight before him. A man, woman and a child, all three bodies long desiccated, lay on the bed together. Beside them on a nightstand, was an empty bottle of sleeping pills. Mike stepped into the room and inspected the bodies a little more. As he did, he saw the large piece of meat missing from the child's left leg and the woman's right arm, as well as the back of the woman and child's head was missing, their dried brains splattered on the wall.

When he looked closer, he saw the man had what looked like dried leather in his mouth, and when Mike was right over the bed, he saw that the man's head had a large gunshot hole on the left side of his head as well. It was easy to figure out what must have happened.

The man, the father probably, had become a zombie and had attacked his wife and child. The wife had managed to shoot the man when they were attacked and then knowing she and the child were doomed, had given the child sleeping pills to kill her, then once the child died, she had put a bullet in her head so she wouldn't rise. Then with her family dead, the wife had placed the father on the bed as well and had taken her own life by eating a bullet.

Mike walked around the bed and found the revolver on the floor the woman had used, but it was empty. He searched for ammunition, and when none could be located, he left the gun. Without ammo it was useless other than as a club.

He might have pondered the fate of the family a little more, but the sunlight shining through the window was waning and he knew he needed to get a move on. Leaving the family of corpses, he stepped back into the hallway, closing the door as he left.

There were two more doors in the hallway; one was a linen closet and the other a child's room. It must have been the room of the child in the other bedroom, he mused.

It was a little girl's room and there, on the floor near the small twin bed, were a pair of dust-covered dolls. Mike was elated at the find. He scooped them up, brushed them off, and used a red sheet off the bed as a sack. He then went through the closet in the room and found dresses and other clothing that would fit his daughters perfectly.

By the time he was finished, the sack was fit to bursting and he had to use another shirt to tie it closed. He tossed it over his shoulder and headed out of the room, feeling good for the first time since his trek began. He went by the kitchen to check it and his luck held. He found a few assorted items to take with him, including a dented can of apricots, a can of beans, some stale crackers and half a bag of rice. Then, way in the back of a top shelf, he found a can of beef stew and was so happy he could cry. After the meager rations he and his family were surviving on, the stew would be a Christmas dinner to remember.

At the front door, he made sure he had everything, and with the machete in his right hand, he used his left and opened the door.

The sack was so big he almost didn't fit through the doorway, but he pulled on it and he slid through. He didn't bother closing the door behind him, as it was too difficult to turn around on the small stoop.

As he walked down the steps and onto the overgrown walkway leading to the street, he never saw the zombie that jumped out of the bushes and sank its teeth into his left wrist.

With a yell of shock and pain, he yanked his arm out of its mouth, blood spraying into the air to dance in the fading rays of sunlight.

The zombie lost its balance and fell to the stone path, right at Mike's feet.

He was so angry he dropped the sack of clothing and toys and swung the machete with both hands on the handle. The blade connected with dead tissue and the head of the ghoul went flying through the air, spinning three times before landing in the tall grass. Even as it disappeared, Mike could hear the teeth continually clacking together.

He fell to his knees and dropped the machete, trying to staunch the flow of blood squirting out of his wrist with his free hand. The wound was bad, real bad.

Like slicing your wrist with a razor blade, the zombie's teeth had torn an artery or vein and the blood was shooting between his fingers no matter how hard he squeezed.

Taking off his belt, he used it as a tourniquet, but even as the blood flow slowed, he knew it was irrelevant. He was bitten, and that could only mean one thing.

But it didn't matter, nothing did but returning home to his family, so he could give them their Christmas presents. He used one of the dresses for the girls as a bandage and wrapped it around the wound, but despite the tourniquet, the bandage was soaked with blood in a matter of minutes.

Shoving the machete into his pants, he picked up the sack and began walking back to his hidden car a half mile away.

It was a hard walk, and by the time he reached the outskirts of town, he was sweating profusely, his shirt a sodden mess of soaked material. A trail of blood drops was behind him, and if anyone was following him, Mike wouldn't be hard to find.

The sun was setting as he reached his car and he fell over the hood and sucked in air, struggling to remain conscious. He wasn't thinking straight anymore, and as fever racked his body thanks to the infectious bite, only one thing was on his mind.

Return home…for Christmas.

It took all his remaining effort to get the sack in the car and for him to follow it. With drooping eyelids and shallow breaths, as well as a complexion that made him look as white as a bed sheet, he managed to get the key into the ignition and start the engine.

Using one hand—ignoring the seeping blood as it soaked into the seat—he backed the car out of its hiding spot and began the drive home, his body going numb as the infection filled him from head to toe.

He would make it, he had to, for his wife, for his girls, he had to get home. For if he didn't, they wouldn't have a merry Christmas.

And if it was the last thing he did in this life, he wanted to give them that.

Sharon was filled with worry.

It was dark out and Mike wasn't home yet.

He'd promised he would be home before it was dark.

She jumped nearly to the ceiling when there was a dull thump at the cabin door. The girls looked up from where they were playing by the fireplace and Sharon told them to stay there after saying, "It's Daddy, he's back, and right on time!"

She dashed to the door, filled with relief that her husband had made it back safely, and with luck, he'd done what he hoped and had found presents for the girls.

Oh, what a wonderful Christmas this would be and now she regretted giving Mike a hard time about leaving.

Without a moment's hesitation, she threw open the door and then stopped cold, a scream on the tip of her tongue as her mouth opened into the shape of an 'O'.

Mike stood in the doorway, swaying back and forth, as if he heard music only for him. He held the red sack of toys and clothes like before, but that was where the picture of normalcy ended.

His clothing was stained a bright red, thanks to arterial spray when the tourniquet had come loose. As he bled out in the car and died, his life's blood had painted him red, making his attire look much like a red suit…a Santa Claus suit.

His face was ashen gray, his eyes now white, the pupil's devoid of color. His free hand reached out for Sharon, the gaping wound where the zombie had taken a chunk out of him still glistening as it reflected the firelight from within the cabin.

The girls had jumped up and ran to their mother's legs, wanting to see what Daddy had brought them, when Mike let out a loud moan. To Sharon and the girls it was unintelligible, but to Mike's dead mind, it was his last attempt at speech as he tried to say, "Merry Christmas."

Sharon broke from her stupor as she uttered, "Oh God no, not now, not like this."

Just as she finished speaking, and before she could so much as try and close the door, to keep out the abomination that was her husband, Mike dropped the sack of goodies and lunged for her.

His hands found Sharon's neck, the one he'd caressed with lips and fingers only a night previous, and now he squeezed as his mouth opened wide to sink his teeth into her tender flesh.

As she stumbled back, Mike followed, and his left foot hit the door, kicking it closed.

The girls screamed, not understanding what was happening, and as Sharon fell to the floor, Mike was on top of her. With the makeshift Christmas tree looking on from the corner, he began to feed, the blood soaking up the firelight and twinkling like lights on a real Christmas tree. The two little girls began to cry, calling out for Mommy and begging Daddy to leave her alone.

Sharon heard none of it, suffering horribly as she died, and still Mike fed on her warm flesh.

Minutes passed, only the slurping of Mike feeding filling the cabin, and the girls sobbing relentlessly as they shook in terror.

Suddenly, Mike stopped feeding and looked up, seeing the two young morsels huddling in the corner of the cabin. Leaving his dead wife, he slowly began to shamble toward the girls as Sharon's corpse slowly began to twitch with renewed life, animating once more as movement filled her corpse.

As Mike leered over his two sobbing children, from behind him Sharon came to her knees and began crawling after him, the warm flesh of the two young girls calling out to her.

The girls, petrified to a state of absolute panic, could only sob and beg, pleading for their parents not to hurt them, but to make things right and protect them from the bad things in the world.

With blood dripping from his chin, Mike reached out for the closest girl, his mouth already open wide for the Christmas feast.

The lone cabin sat in the middle of the woods, far from civilization. Only a few crickets marred the silence, as well as a night bird or two calling out.

Suddenly, from the cabin, shrieks of the two children filled the night, causing the night birds to fly away, startled. The crickets stopped and the forest fell completely silent, with the exception of the girls' screams echoing from within the cabin.

In time, the screams faded, and all was quiet once more.

THE LAST CHRISTMAS

Thomas Jurgensen wandered the cold lonely street, wrapped in nothing but rags. The snow on the ground was two feet deep and he could feel the ice crystals inside his worn boots.

All around him were the signs of a dead neighborhood, the same as every other one he'd passed through in the twelve months since the dead began to walk and swarmed across the world like locusts.

Stopping in the middle of the street, he stared at the house to his right. It was a standard two-story house with a two car garage and a large picture window in front. In that window, Christmas decorations still hung, the scotch tape holding the cardboard cutouts of Santa and his reindeer firm.

After a full year of hanging in the window, the sun beating on the facades, the colors were now washed out and only the dark lines of the shapes could be seen.

On the front lawn, buried under two feet of snow, three unlit plastic reindeer frolicked. Their white skeletal frames were once lit up, but now they truly looked like skeletons.

Hanging askew on the roof, a life-size sleigh clung to its moorings. Exposed to the winds and weather, it wouldn't be long before the sleigh was forced off the roof to crash to the ground below.

Thomas shook his head in sadness, wondering how it could have come to this.

It wasn't a long story how the dead came to walk, it was quite simple actually.

A cure to the common cold, it was heralded as. Finally, no more runny noses and chests full of phlegm. But the cure hadn't been tested as well as it should be, the drug companies in a rush to get it on the market. To make up for the loss of cough syrup and allergy medicines, the price of the cure was incredible, but nine out of ten people were happy to pay it.

So when the first fatality was admitted into a local hospital, no one gave the woman much thought. At least until the patient died and returned as a living corpse, sinking her teeth into the nurse administering over her.

From there it was a domino effect, and in the blink of an eye, a year later, Thomas was standing on a holiday festive street in the middle of Nowhere, USA, shivering in the cold. The wind blowing in from the north felt like it would freeze him to the bone, and he turned and headed for the ranch house.

All around him were the frozen corpses of zombies, each as stiff as the day it had frozen months ago. But Thomas knew when spring came they would thaw out and be free to roam once more.

There was a time when he would have tried to destroy them, to chop off their heads and break their legs as they lay helpless in the snow. But months ago he had finally given up. There were just too damn many to destroy.

So now he used the winter time to stock up on whatever he could find, and when spring arrived, he would hole up some-where until winter returned.

The front door of the house was locked, so he went around to the back. This door was locked too and it was a heavy wooden fabrication. But there were more ways to enter the house and he found it by using a basement window. After kicking out the glass with the heel of his worn boot, he scurried in like a worm sliding into its hole.

The basement was dark and dingy, but was slightly warmer than outside.

That made Thomas nervous. Anywhere the temperature wasn't below freezing, a zombie could be lying in wait.

He remembered the last time he found a zombie in a house.

It was three weeks ago to the day. He had climbed in through an open window to find the bedroom door leading to the rest of the house empty. Upon opening the door, he found himself standing face to face with a dead man in a Santa Claus suit. With the door closed. The rest of the house had managed to stay above freezing.

But Santa wasn't as jolly as days past. This Santa had a massive hole in his throat, a missing arm and intestines hanging like dangling rope from his abdomen.

As the dead Santa raised its one remaining hand, Thomas heard the tinkle of jingle bells, the three red bells sewed to the sleeve of the red suit. As the zombie moaned, the bells jangled, and Thomas slammed the door in the festive ghoul's face.

As the holiday zombie pounded on the bedroom door, Thomas had climbed out of the house to find another hiding place.

So now here he was again, inside a house searching for anything useful. Empty cardboard boxes sat on his left, the words **XMAS STUFF** written on them in black marker. He chuckled slightly at the sight. Of course they were empty. All the decorations were set up around the home. It was like this in every house he went to. When the outbreak began, it had been three days to Christmas, and though the world died, at least it left a festive corpse.

The basement was relatively empty, though he found an old claw hammer on a dented and rusted metal shelf. The hammer was better than nothing, so he tossed away the cracked bat he'd been using, knowing the bat's days were numbered. Swinging the hammer once or twice to get a feel for it, he turned and began climbing the steps to the first floor.

The door was locked, but his new acquisition saw him through. With the door lock now splintered and lying on the top step, he pushed the door in and waited for signs of trouble. He was confident that any zombies would have been attracted to the noise he made breaking the lock. He waited for a full minute, and when still nothing arrived to attack him, he stepped inside the kitchen.

It was a kitchen like any other he'd seen over the past year. A snowman cookie jar sat on its side on the counter, even the crumbs now gone. Christmas potholders hung from the cabinets and small statues, five inches in height, sat on the edge of the stove, while salt and pepper shakers of elves lay on their side in the middle of the kitchen table.

That was the only sense of normalcy in the kitchen, however, as the rest was a maelstrom of tossed aside empty boxes and brown, dirty dishes. When he reached the kitchen sink, he turned up his nose as the sight greeting him. A large, dried turd, human by the size and shape, lay in the bottom of the sink, and Thomas had to wonder what kind of human would feel the need to climb up onto the counter to defecate like that. But he'd seen worse in his travels and he moved on.

As Thomas searched the cupboards, they were as bare as the preverbal old woman in a shoe. When he was through searching, not finding so much as a crumb, thanks to the looters before him, he went into the living room.

He had his fingers crossed about what he might find there, and sure enough, he was correct.

In the center of the large living room, stood a brown Christmas tree, all the needles now on the floor. Ornaments still hung from it, but as the once fresh tree was now long dead, the branches looking unappealing and ugly in their bareness.

The tree was like the world now. A few pretty baubles on its surface, but underneath, it was dead and rotting.

But that wasn't what Thomas was looking for. It was what was below the tree that had him coming to the living room in the first place.

Below the dried and brown tree, a fire hazard in the waiting, sat the presents of this home's family, every one still wrapped with care a year ago.

For some reason, looters didn't think to check the presents, only going to the obvious places, such as the kitchen, pantry and medicine cabinets in the bathrooms.

But Thomas had figured out long ago that there were hidden treasures to be found sitting under desiccated Christmas trees. Setting the hammer down, he dropped to his knees and bean ripping open the presents.

To: Timmy, Love, Mom and Dad, the first one had written on the wrapping paper, and when Thomas opened it, he saw it was a video game. He tossed it aside and went for the next one.

To: Sally, Love, Mom and Dad, the next card said and this one had a pink ribbon on the corner.

Thomas ripped the ribbon off and tore into the present, to an outsider looking like a kid on Christmas morning. All he got for his trouble was a new cell phone.

Beyond worthless, he thought, as he tossed the box aside.

But this had happened before which was why looters didn't bother.

Thomas picked up the next one. *To: Daddy, From: Timmy,* was on a homemade card. There was a drawing there, too. Timmy had used crayons to draw Santa and his reindeer as they flew across a happy town. Thomas ripped the card off and threw it behind him, then he ripped open the present like a hungry dog and cried out in relief to see what was inside.

It was a summer sausage gift set, complete with two blocks of cheese, mustard, and crackers. The perfect present to give a man who needs nothing but you have to give him something.

Ravenous beyond imagining, Thomas tore into the package and feasted on the sausage. Though it was processed meat that he would have shunned a year earlier, now it tasted like the finest New York sirloin. He ate half the sausage and then a quarter of the cheese, devouring half the crackers with it. Then, his stomach feeling better, he continued opening presents.

He went through four more, one was a new IPod for the little girl, the other was an action figure from some Japanese cartoon for the boy. The second to last was a sweater for the mother, cashmere if he was right. Not worried about fashion sense, he set it aside to take with him. Warm was warm and there was no one to impress anymore. And besides, the dead didn't judge you, they only wanted to eat you.

The last present was addressed to the father, and when Thomas opened it up, he gasped in happiness to see a brand new Browning Hi-power, complete with a box of ammunition. This was the find of a lifetime. And to think, it had been sitting here for all this time, ignored by others!

After loading the gun, he felt so much better, knowing he wouldn't have to get close to an attacker to defend himself.

Going to the front door, he stepped outside and grabbed some snow from the front porch, eating it. It melted in his mouth and he sighed, washing the salty taste of the sausage and crackers from his palate. At least with the snow he had all the water he could ever want, but he still needed food. At least now, for a day or so, he had both.

When he had his fill, he closed the door and went back into the living room. This time he noticed the rest of the holiday decorations spread out across the room.

Near the front window were two animatronic statues of Santa and Mrs. Claus. Both were covered in a layer of dust and hadn't been on in more than a year. Off to the right was a fireplace, the family stockings hanging in front like a classic Christmas card. Two large ones had Mom and Dad on them, while the other two had the names Timmy and Sally.

Made sense to Thomas, especially after ripping open the presents and reading the cards.

On the walls were holiday cardboard cutouts similar to the faded ones on the front window. Rudolph, Santa, and Frosty all smiled down onto the living room, where once a happy family had laughed, loved and played together.

That had Thomas wondering where the family might be. Had they evacuated like so many families had in the beginning? He felt for them if they did. The rescue stations had quickly become concentration camps, where death and sickness ruled with an iron fist.

Luckily Thomas had been alone when it all started. He was already a widower and he and his wife had never had kids. All his family was either dead or estranged when the world crumbled. Which was why it had been easy for him to adapt, as he had no one to worry about but himself.

With a full stomach and the inside of the house much warmer than outside, he felt his exhaustion sneaking up on him, and he decided it was time to get some rest. He did a few things before he slept, however. The first was to use the bathroom, not caring about his waste being left behind in the empty bowl. The second was to use one of the kitchen chairs to block the basement door from opening. If he thought to enter the house that way, so could another. He hadn't seen many other people in this part of the town, but one could never be too careful. At least if one wanted to stay alive, that is.

When the house was as secure as it could be, he went back to the living room and dropped down on the dusty couch. There was a dust-covered throw blanket on the back cushion and he pulled it down onto him.

Then, snug and comfortable, he drifted off into sleep, into a world where Christmas didn't equal death, and if you saw Santa Claus on the street, he wasn't going to try and rip your throat out.

Thomas came awake with a startled groan. He'd heard something, the question was: What was it?

Always on the run, he had learned to sleep lightly, and no matter how tired he was, he always managed to do this.

So he knew something had woken him from his troubled rest.

He sat up and could barely see, darkness having descended almost completely. Checking his wristwatch, he saw he had been asleep for almost four hours.

His bladder required attention and he silently padded to the bathroom, took care of business, and then proceeded to go back to the living room.

That was when he heard the noise again. It was a scratching sound, like a dog wanting out and its claws brushing the door.

It was coming from the second floor. He hadn't checked the second floor, not feeling the need. The gun was in his waistband, but he went back to retrieve the hammer, then, as well armed as one could be in this day and age, he began to climb the stairs leading to the second floor.

Halfway up, he paused to study the family photos hanging on the wall. There was a small fixed window that allowed light in and the wan illumination was enough for Thomas to see the smiling faces in the pictures. A man, woman and two children, a boy and a girl, looked out at him, with cheerful eyes and wide smiles. This must be the family that lived here, the two children named Timmy and Sally.

They looked so happy and Thomas couldn't help but feel his heartstrings tugged just a little.

But then the scratching could be heard again and he was brought back to the here and now. He reached the top landing, and he walked down the small hallway, peering into each room as he went. There was the parents' bedroom, the dust thick with disuse, the floor void of fresh footprints; the bathroom was empty and the first child's bedroom was empty also.

That left the last room at the end of the hall.

The door was closed and the name **TIMMY** was on a small sign tacked to the middle of the door.

Thomas stepped closer and placed his ear to the door.

There it was again, that scratching noise.

While there was absolutely no reason for him to open the door, he felt his curiosity get the better of him. It didn't hurt that he now had a gun and if there was any true danger he could shoot the problem and then leave.

For once he felt in control and he was damned if he would run away.

He wanted to know what was in the room, and had been inside for a year or so.

So with treacle-like slowness, he reached out to the doorknob with his free hand.

Turning it careful, he pushed the door open and took a step back, lest a hidden ghoul attack him.

But there was no attack, nothing happened. But the scratching began to grow louder.

When he was sure it was safe, he raised the gun and stepped into the room.

Immediately he was blasted by the rank odor of stale death and the reason for this aroma was apparent the instant he entered the room.

There were two zombie children, a boy and girl, only the clothing allowing Thomas to know this for sure. Both were tied by the necks like dogs, their small bodies far too weak to ever hope to break their leashes.

Below them, on the floor, were the remains of two adult bodies. There was no meat left and the skeletons pieces that were till intact looked chewed on, like someone had been gnawing on them for some time.

The heads were tossed to the side, the skulls empty, as if a small hand had plunged into the neck cavity of each to scoop out the juicy brains within.

Thomas took the room in at a glance. There were pieces of rotted, dried meat off to the side, and a few of the pieces looked as if they may have been human.

It wasn't too hard for Thomas to piece together what must have happened.

Somehow, the two children had been infected and had turned into the walking dead. The parents hadn't the heart to destroy their offspring and so had penned them up, tying them up like wild animals. Then the kids had been fed a diet of raw meat and human when possible. But something had gone wrong, perhaps the kids getting the drop on their parents. And then the parents had become a meal for their children.

The two little zombies snarled and hissed at him, their drawn visages basically nothing more than human skulls wrapped in dried skin. The small zombies hadn't eaten for a very long time and were ravenous for human flesh.

They were an odd sight, the two wearing festive holiday clothing, though now it was covered in brown and crusting blood from meals long past. The boy wore a yellow sweater with Santa Claus on the front, while the girl wore a blue sweatshirt with a snowman with a black top hat.

Frosty, had to be, Thomas figured.

Thomas stared at the kids and then at the gun in his hand. In the end, he decided he didn't need to waste two bullets on them. They were trapped and small and he had the hammer.

Shoving the gun in into his waistband, he raised the hammer and stepped closer to the boy. He was less than a foot away, but the leash was short and the boy couldn't reach him. He raised the hammer high and then brought it down hard; the skull cracking like it was made of plaster. The boy dropped to the floor, gray brains seeping out the hole in his head.

Thomas barely felt anything as he turned to face the girl. She hissed and snapped; her hands out in front of her. The leash was taut as she stretched to reach him.

He laughed, feeling powerful, knowing it was petty, but still relishing his power. After a year of being on the run by these *things*, it was nice to be in the driver's seat for a change.

Almost casually, he raised the hammer again, his attention barely on the task at hand. He was already thinking about eating the rest of the summer sausage with mustard.

His carelessness was his undoing, as he had learned a long time ago any zombie was a danger, no matter how helpless it might seem.

As he raised the hammer and looked away for the briefest of seconds, the leash holding the zombie girl snapped, and she came at him with mouth open wide.

He brought the hammer down, but only grazed her head, the blow breaking her clavicle instead of her skull. But the little girl could have cared less. Before Thomas could stop her or jump away, she sank her brown teeth into his right leg, just above his knee joint.

He screamed in pain and anger and raised the hammer again, this time his attention fully on the killing. The hammer cracked her skull like a melon and the point of the hammer sank halfway into the small skull, the girl twitching on the end of the hammer like she was being electrocuted.

Her teeth clamped down in her death throes and tore a two inch size chunk of flesh from his leg. Howling in pain, he kicked the corpse away from him and dropped the hammer.

The girl was very dead now, the small body dropping onto the two skeletons of her parents.

Moaning in pain, Thomas left the bedroom, slamming the door behind him. He wasn't cursing himself as he wasn't thinking that far ahead. Instead, he rushed to the bathroom and ripped open the vanity.

He found what he needed, but it was in short supply after looters had taken what they wanted, but he ripped open his pant leg and cleaned the wound. Then he bandaged it.

With nothing left to do, he went downstairs and sat on the couch, his leg throbbing with each beat of his heart.

He still didn't want to admit it, but he knew what that little zombie girl had given him for Christmas.

A death sentence.

Though he was hurting and upset, eventually he fell back to sleep, though now his dreams were plagued with even more zombies, and by the end he found he was one of them.

When he woke up his leg was numb, and when he checked under the bandage, he saw the wound had festered. It had already started and there would be no stopping it.

He finished off the sausage and cheese, sucking every last ounce of mustard from the packet. He wasn't worried about eating it all. He didn't need to save it anymore and at least this way he would die with a relatively full stomach.

Then he sat and waited, only getting up to use the bathroom and eat some snow.

By the second day, he didn't bother to do that, and the last time he needed to pee, he'd said the hell with it and had simply leaned over the edge of the couch and urinated on the floor. Hell, it wasn't his house and in another day he wouldn't be alive to care.

That night he was holding on to life by his willpower alone. He knew if he passed out that would be it.

And he knew for a fact he didn't want to become one of *them*.

He picked up the Browning and held it in his grip. He remembered just a day or so ago when he'd found it, and how lucky he'd felt.

In fact, he had been so happy it had been just like Christmas to him, what with finding the gun and the summer sausage. He wasn't sure, but he was pretty sure December 25th was close, the anniversary of the outbreak the same week.

So it was Christmas again, albeit a rather lonely one for him.

As he placed the gun to his temple and closed his eyes, he mumbled one last sentence.

"Some Merry Christmas."

He held the gun there for almost ten minutes, not having the courage to go through with it. But then he felt a sharp pain in his chest, one that filled him with agony.

That pain gave him the courage to do what had to be done.

He squeezed the trigger.

A VERY DEAD CHRISTMAS

Welcome, dear reader, to a tale of Christmas, where things aren't always as they seem.

What do we mean? Read on and find out.

* * *

"Well, everyone, this is the last of the reindeer meat," Mrs. Claus said as she sat the platter full of steaming meat on the center of the dinner table. "All the rest have become zombies." It was exactly one month until Christmas Day.

"Are you sure, Martha?" Santa Claus asked, his mouth already salivating at the aroma of the cooked meat. He was a fat bastard; there was no doubt about it. In the stories, he was described as round and jolly, but in reality, he was simply one fat mother-fucker. He had a glandular problem, and no matter how much he dieted, he just gained weight.

Not that this helped during the present food shortage that had hit the North Pole since the zombie apocalypse happened more than a year ago.

Martha sat down next to her husband, then let her eyes glance over the remaining elves sitting with them. "Yes, I'm afraid this is the last of our food."

There was Happy. "This sucks," Happy said, a perpetual frown on his lips. He was actually the absolute opposite of happy, which was where he got his name. It was supposed to be 'ironic.'

Next was Skinny. "Not to me, I love deer steak." He licked his lips at the sight of the still-sizzling meat. Skinny was almost as fat as Santa, only a few feet shorter. Once more, his name was sup-posed to be 'ironic.'

The next elf tried to grab a piece of steak but Martha slapped his hand with a ladle. "Not yet, Handsome Joe, we need to say Grace."

Of course, if you the reader are getting the whole theme here, Handsome Joe wasn't handsome at all. The best way to describe Handsome Joe was to take an asshole, stretch it so that it was the size of a face, then add some squinty eyes, a crooked nose, and a thin gash of a mouth. Handsome Joe was butt ugly, and that's not being 'ironic,' that was a fact.

The next elf was called Steve.

Yes, that's right: Steve.

What was wrong with him? What made his name Steve of all things?

How the fuck do I know? Steve is a good name, and that was what his mother named him. See? Fooled ya, didn't I? I bet you thought he was gonna have some kind of defect, like being a mutant or something. Well, the worst thing about Steve was that he was Republican, but we won't hold that over him—much.

"Hey, I heard that. I'm not Republican, I'm Libertarian."

Oh, sorry, about that Steve. Let's just say you're short and leave it at that.

"Fuck you, pal. I'm not short, I'm just not as tall as everyone else."

We're getting off track here, Steve, shut up and leave us alone. So, back to the story.

"Jerk," Steve muttered.

Oh yeah, and the rest of the elves names were Big Dick, Taint, Little Ripper, Mustache Ride and Smells Like Fish (or Fishy for short) and Slut, a female elf—you can try and figure out why Slut is named this on your own time. But here's a freebie. Slut loved to fuck.

"Are you going to say Grace this time, Santa?" Steve asked as he sat in his chair, waiting to eat. He was very well-mannered, and though his stomach grumbled, he had enough dignity to wait till it was time to eat.

"Grace?" Santa asked. "Fuck that shit. I'm fucking starving over here." He nodded to Martha. "Hey, babe, give me the biggest piece, and let's get down to eating. We can say Grace 'after' we've eaten." To emphasize his words, he leaned to the side and let out a mighty fart.

Being magic, the fart plumed out like a dark cloud and a face appeared. The cloud-face looked at each of the diners, winked once, then floated off to the ceiling, where it slowly dispersed.

"Well, that was a nice change of pace," Mrs. Claus said. "At least this fart was polite, not like some of the others." She glared at Santa, as if it was his fault when the farts would float from person to person, hovering around their face to let the person get a good whiff, and only then would it disperse.

"Hey, don't look at me," Santa defended. "My farts have a mind of their own. I don't control them once they leave my ass."

Martha sighed. "I declare, you're such a pig. Where the stories came from of you being fun, jolly, and sweet is a mystery."

Santa shoved a piece of deer steak into his mouth, then let out a loud burp. "I got a good publicist, babe. It's all in the image, you see, not what really is. Spread enough info around about someone and eventually some of it will stick like shit to a wall."

Martha sighed as she cut into her piece of steak. The elves were eating, too, and had been since Santa had farted.

Martha nibbled on her steak as she looked across the table at the others. This was all that was left of the North Pole residents. The rest of the elves had either died of starvation or had taken it upon themselves to venture out in search of help and supplies. Of course, the North Pole was isolated, so there was no help to be found. No doubt, those elves had frozen to death. She felt bad for them, but selfishly was glad they had left. At least that had made the remaining food stock last longer. It wasn't long before the reindeer were being slaughtered for their meat. Some had become zombies, but the ones that hadn't, had still suffered a fate as bad or worse than being zombified—they became food for the survivors.

Santa inhaled the rest of his steak, then he leaned over the table, and with a fork in each hand, snatched the remaining meat from each of the elves' dishes.

"Hey, what the fuck, Santa, I was eating that!" Happy snapped, angry that he'd lost his meal. The other elves looked the same but only Happy had the balls to actually say something.

Santa stood up, while still shoving the stolen meat into his mouth. He dropped the forks and spread his hands wide, challenging Happy. "What, Happy, you got something to fucking say to me? Come on, ya little shit, I'll squash you like a goddamn bug. You think you can take me on, bitch? Huh?" His eyes roamed over the others. "You think any of you can fucking take me? Then bring it on, motherfuckers! I'm the fucking boss around here, and don't you little pissants forget it." He let out another mighty fart and when it plumed up beside him, he directed it to go right at Happy and the other elves.

Santa turned and walked out of the room, grumbling about how this was 'His house,' and no one better try to take it from him. Martha gently placed her fork down and crossed her arms over her ample bosom. "I knew he could control them, no matter how much he denied it."

Happy was waving his hands around his head, trying to get the fart to dissipate, but the cloud just moved to the other elves, who sat still and took it. When the cloud finally rose to the ceiling and faded away, Steve pushed off from his chair and stood up. Of course, being so damn short, it still looked like was he sitting. But you get the point. He stood for dramatic effect, and though it didn't matter shit to the others, it made Steve feel good.

"We need to do something about that fat fuck." His eyes went right to Mrs. Claus. "Ma'am, I know he's your husband, but we can't keep going on like this. Maybe he won't hurt you, but the rest of us aren't as lucky. He'll kill us if he wants, and there will be no one to stop him from doing it."

Martha sighed wearily. "I know, Steve, but what do you want me to do? I still love the big jerk. He's just cranky because he's not getting enough to eat." She smiled at each of the elves. "You'll see, boys, once he gets some decent food in him, everything will go back to normal around here." She stood up. "Now, why don't you all go and attend to your chores. Someone needs to clean up the stable too; take care of all the blood from the last deer that was killed."

The elves, all grumbling to themselves, left the table, but Handsome Joe stopped and walked around the table to look up at Mrs. Claus. "You said that was the last of the food, is that right?"

She nodded down at him. She had become used to his butt-ugly face.

"So then, if there's no more food, what are we going to eat? What's Santa going to eat so that he'll calm down?"

Martha patted Handsome Joe's shoulder gently, like a mother to a son. "Don't you worry about that, dear. Precautions are being taken. Santa has a contingency plan in place for a situation like this."

"He does?"

"Yes, dear, he does. Now get going and go do your chores. At least if anything, it'll take your mind off of food for a while."

"Oh, okay, Ma'am, I guess you're right." He turned and walked away.

Martha watched him leave. She crossed her arms on the table and rested her head on her arms. Closing her eyes, she sighed yet again. She found herself doing that a lot lately. There was a lot to sigh about. No more food, Santa ready to explode, and the world having collapsed thanks to the dead walking. Things had never been as dire as they were right now.

Four days later.

All the elves shuffled into the dining room, hungry and exhausted. Due to the apocalypse, they were down to a fraction of the elf power they once had, and running the North Pole took a lot of hands.

There were the factories to keep going. Sure, the world might have been ruled by zombies, but toys still had to be made. Santa demanded it, and what Santa wanted, Santa got. He figured sooner or later the dead would be put down and then it would be business as usual, what with the gift giving, and the Ho-Ho-Ho shit he was known for.

As everyone sat down, only Santa and Mrs. Claus having not yet arrived, Handsome Joe looked around the table. He counted elves and came up one short. "Hey, guys, has anyone seen Skinny around?"

Steve looked over where Skinny would normally sit and he shrugged as he took in the empty chair. "No, I haven't. Come to think of it, I haven't seen him since yesterday." He leaned forward and made eye contact with some of the other elves. "Any of you guys seen Skinny around lately?"

Big Dick stopped talking to Little Ripper and glanced at Steve. "Who gives a shit about Skinny? The lazy, fat fuck is probably sleeping somewhere. Wherever he went, leave him be. More food for the rest of us."

"Yeah," Happy added. "The guy eats enough for three people; if he's not here, that's more for us."

Steve shrugged again, deciding he was going nowhere with the others. Handsome Joe frowned but said nothing. Maybe Skinny was sleeping somewhere, but one thing about the fat elf that everyone knew, the guy never missed a meal.

Santa came strolling into the room and sat down at the head of the table. He took one look at the talking elves and slammed his hand on the table, making the dishes and glasses jump an inch before coming back down to rattle for a second. "Enough talking! Shut the fuck up."

Most of the elves stopped talking but Handsome Joe was on a roll, and he kept going. When the others went silent, Handsome Joe's voice grew louder, and for the first few seconds, he didn't realize he was the only one talking, but he quickly figured it out when Santa roared, "Handsome Joe, how would you like a candy cane shoved up your ass? I said for everyone to shut up!"

Handsome Joe went silent and he looked down at the table. "Sorry, Santa, I wasn't paying attention."

Santa only growled in reply, mumbling something about butt-ugly elves. He shifted in his seat, as if he was daring someone else to speak. When he was satisfied he had control of the room, he leaned forward in his chair and slapped his hand on the table again. "Okay, so someone give me an update on how things are going around here."

"I'll do it," Steve said and stood up. He pulled a sheaf of papers from a hidden pocket and unrolled them, then began reading. "We're out of food, there's nothing to eat but ice and more ice. The factories are almost at a standstill due to not enough hands to work them. Communication with the outside world has gone completely silent; we haven't heard any kind of a transmission for over two weeks, and Skinny seems to have disappeared." He folded the papers and sat back down. Some of the elves began to mumble amongst themselves, but a glare from Santa silenced them once more.

"The factories need to keep running, Steve, you all know that," Santa explained. "We make toys here, and sooner or later we'll get back to normal, then those toys will be delivered. As for the food situation…" He managed a smile, which looked more like a grimace thanks to his overgrown white beard. "I procured some food for us. Martha is going to bring it in shortly, but until then, we need to make a plan for the future so that we're all still here when it comes."

Santa began laying out plans he'd come up with, how they needed to be strong and have hope that things would get better. A few elves asked some questions, but Santa mostly talked in circles, not really answering the questions, and sometimes actually twisting their questions back on them by asking a few of his own.

Steve was about to call Santa on his bullshit, no matter what the fat man's wrath might be, when Mrs. Claus entered the room, carrying a large, ceramic tureen filled with something brown. The aroma quickly filled the room, making all the elves and Santa salivate hungrily.

"Wow, Mrs. Claus, that smells fantastic," Handsome Joe said.

"I'm starving," Santa added, as the tureen was placed in the center of the table. All the elves tried to get a look inside the large bowl, but they were too short to see. Big Dick hopped up on his chair but a glare from Santa made him sit back down.

"Now, now, boys, there's enough for everyone," Mrs. Claus said with a smile.

"But we haven't eaten for days," Steve said, licking his lips with a rather dry tongue.

"Then give me your bowl so you can eat now," she replied and reached out for his bowl. Steve handed it to her, and a few seconds later, he had a steaming bowl of what resembled stew before him. Mrs. Claus quickly ladled out heaping bowls to the other elves, then Santa as well. Santa's bowl was double the size of the elves' dishes—not that they would have said anything.

Without waiting for anyone, Santa dug in, a lot of the stew getting in his beard. He ignored it, shoveling the food into his mouth hungrily.

The elves barely noticed, for they too, were eating with abandon. It had been days since they'd eaten solid food, as only water had been their diet, whether it was liquid or frozen, many of them chewing ice to stave off hunger.

Steve ate as well but not with as much gusto. As he chewed on a piece of unidentifiable meat, his spoon moved the stew around in his bowl. The meat was fatty, very fatty, and had a taste similar to pork. Now, where had Mrs. Claus found pork up at the North Pole?

"Say, Mrs. Claus," Steve said, "Where did you say you got this meat?"

"She got it at the 'shut the fuck up' store," Santa snapped. "If you don't want to eat it I'll be happy to eat yours." He reached for Steve's bowl but the elf slid it away from his gasp.

"No, Santa, I'm fine, I was just curious."

Santa licked his bowl clean, then held it out to his wife for another serving. "Good, because there's barely enough food to go around now, so if you don't want it, there's plenty who do. Isn't that right, boys?" he asked the other elves, who all replied in different ways, whether by nodding profusely or just voicing their agreement.

The rest of the meal was quiet, only the sounds of slurping and chewing filling the air. When all the stew was gone, Santa leaned back and rubbed his giant belly, burping once, then farting. The fart floated up and smiled to everyone, and with a wave floated away. Santa was content so didn't feel the need to send his fart at any of the elves. "Martha, baby, you did wonders with that meat. Outstanding, woman."

"Thank you, dear," she said and stood up and began gathering dishes. "Slut, will you give me a hand, please?"

The female elf did as asked, piling the bowls together and carrying them into the nearby kitchen.

"Okay, you assholes," Santa snapped. "You've all been fed, now back to work."

The elves began to file out, each smacking their lips and talking about how good the meal had been. The meat had been fatty, but it had still been delicious. Steve was the last to leave. He paused for a second, and asked, "I still don't understand where Mrs. Claus got the meat for that stew. You said all the reindeer are gone, and there are no other animals around us, and if that's so then…"

Santa rose to his full height and walked over to Steve; the word 'dwarfing' the small elf came to mind as the fat man towered over the short elf. "Steve, you've always been difficult. Now, do you mind telling me why when you were starving, and food was put before you, instead of being thankful, you have to question it all?"

"No, it's not that, Santa, it's just…"

"Exactly. Food has been provided, so just shut the fuck up and be grateful. Now get the fuck out of here and go back to work with the others." Santa cracked his knuckles, the gesture clear. *Get moving or get bitch-slapped.*

Slut popped her head out of the kitchen and she smiled at Steve. He was the only elf she hadn't fucked, and no matter how much she tried, Steve just wasn't interested. She figured he was gay. He wasn't, he just didn't want to stick his small dick where he knew everyone else had already been. Even Santa had taken a whack at that small snatch, or so the rumors around the Pole went.

With nothing else to do, Steve turned and left the dining room, his head shaking in frustration. He knew something was up, a mystery that needed to be solved, but with Santa hovering over him threateningly, he knew it was a mystery that would have to wait.

"Man, I gotta take a massive shit," Santa said to no one in particular. He picked up the North Pole Times and waddled off to the bathroom, a few farts popping out of his ass as he walked. They all floated away, not having any direction given to them by their master.

Steve went off to the factory to see how things were going.

Okay, let's keep this thing moving, we don't want you to get bored. So let's jump ahead a few weeks. Three and a half weeks to be specific. Like at the beginning of the story, everyone was gathered around the dinner table, only there was not as many people as when the story first began.

Steve was still there, and so was Slut, and so were Mrs. Claus and Santa, but the elf population had dwindled even more.

Big Dick was gone, and had been for weeks, and so was Little Ripper. Mustache Ride had disappeared a little over a week ago, and Taint and Smells Like Fish — or Fishy — to his friends, had been missing for two days.

Steve didn't like it at all. Worse, the stew was coming more regularly for dinner, but each time he tried to question Santa or Mrs. Claus on its origin, all he got was threats and changes of the subject.

In fact, Santa looked healthier than ever, and Steve was sure the fat fuck had put on some weight over the past few weeks. No, something stunk at the North Pole, and he was going to figure it out once and for all.

Maybe if Steve had been a little smarter he would have put two and two together by now. We're sure you, the reader, have figured out what's been happening.

"Hey, I heard that, you hack. I have figured it out, but I need proof before I can confront Santa with it," Steve snapped.

Oh really? Then what are you waiting for?

"Just you wait and see. I've got a plan." Steve did, too. When dinner was over, he gathered the remaining elves at the factory after closing and explained what he had in mind. He also explained his theory about Santa killing the elves and feeding them back to the remaining elves as dinner.

"Are you for real?" Happy asked, a large puss on his lips. "You think Santa has been killing us and Mrs. Claus is serving us up in her stew?"

"That's impossible," Slut added. "Mrs. Claus would never do that."

"I agree with Slut," Handsome Joe agreed. "She's too sweet to do something so horrible.

"Yeah, "Happy said. "Besides, if that was true, then that means we've been eating our friends." He blanched. "That's not something I want to think about."

"What don't you want to think about?" Steve asked. "That they tasted damn good, a lot like pork, or that they've been getting slaughtered one by one by the two people we once trusted."

"Neither," Handsome Joe said, frowning. "Ugh, I can still taste dinner. If what you say is true, then who did we just eat?"

"If I had to guess, I would say it was Fishy," Steve said.

Happy nodded, though he was looking sick. "Yeah, makes sense. The stew did taste a little fishy, come to think of it." He turned and vomited into a trashcan. "Oh, shit, I can't believe I just said that, or just ate that meal."

"But this might all be a big misunderstanding," Slut pleaded. "You might be wrong, Steve."

"That's why we need to get into Mrs. Claus kitchen and see what's going on. Haven't you noticed how no one is allowed in there alone?"

"But I help her wash the dishes all the time," Slut said.

"Yes, but that's after the meal, 'after' she's had a chance to clean up anything suspicious."

Slut considered that and it did make sense. Whenever she was helping Mrs. Claus, there had never been any of the meat lying out, and the large refrigerator was always locked. She hadn't given it much thought at the time, but now that Steve was calling attention to it, Mrs. Claus had been acting rather secretive. "Steve's right, guys, I don't want to believe it, but I think he's right."

Happy scowled. "So even if he is doing what you're saying, what the fuck are we supposed to do about it?"

Steve grinned rather evilly. "Simple. We get even."

So here we are again. To keep the story moving, let's just go to some cliff notes, all right?

Steve led the others into the kitchen, a crowbar in his hands. He broke the lock off the refrigerator and low and behold, can you guess what they found?

That's right. Elf bits. Mustache Ride's severed head was on the middle shelf in a pan, and a bucket of small intestines was on the bottom shelf. A pan on the top shelf held Big Dick's dick, and no one wanted to think about what 'that' was going to be used for. Smells Like Fish was present too, but the only thing truly there to identify him was the severed arm they found in the salad crisper. See, there was a tattoo on it, one of a marlin on a hook. Fishy had gotten it years ago, on account of his name. He'd told everyone if he owned the name then it became his, and no one could use it to tease him. No one had really cared one way or the other, but the tattoo was still a hell of a way to know what part belonged to whom.

"That fucking fat bastard," Happy hissed as he stared at the contents of the fridge.

Slut backed away, a hand to her mouth in abject horror. She hadn't really believed what Steve had said, that is, not until this exact moment.

"So…w…what do we do now?" Handsome Joe asked as he sat on a chair and stared at the floor. He wanted to wash his eyes, scrub his mind of the images of his friends cut up like meat in a butcher shop.

Steve walked over to the butcher table across the room, the table now clean of blood. But Steve knew that only hours ago, one of his friends had been there, the small body lying on the table as Santa or Mrs. Claus had hacked and cut and sliced and diced the meat into bite-sized chunks for stew. There was a sharp cleaver on the table. Steve picked it up, holding it with both hands, as it was rather large for his small form. "We finish this," he snarled.

Santa had been dreaming of fucking supermodels when he was pulled from his slumber. His eyes snapped open, and he immediately knew something was terribly wrong. For one thing, he couldn't move his arms, and when he tried to move, he found that wasn't going to happen either.

"What the fu…" he began, but was silenced immediately by a slap to his chubby face.

"Shut up, Santa, you're not in charge anymore," Steve hissed.

Santa gazed up at the face of Steve in the gloom of his bedroom. Behind Steve stood Handsome Joe, Slut and Happy. For once, Happy actually looked 'happy.' Santa moved his head to the side to see that his wife was missing. "Where's Marth…" he began, but once more was cut off by a slap to the face.

"She's dead, fatso, and you'll be joining her soon enough," Steve said.

Santa's eyes went wide and it took less than a heartbeat for his look of confusion to turn into one of anger. "Why, you little fuck. Let me go right now and I promise to make yours and the others' deaths quick, instead of slowly like you all deserve."

Steve stepped a little to the right and Santa was able to see directly behind the small elf. He saw a large form on the floor, and it took only a moment for him to realize it was Mrs. Claus. She was dead, there was no doubt about it. There was a large candy cane sticking out of her right eye.

"That's to make sure she doesn't come back again," Steve said, answering Santa's unanswered question. "She tried to stop us; we had no choice."

Santa began struggling with his bonds again, but the elves had made sure he was good and secured. Santa wasn't going free unless the elves wanted him to.

But they had underestimated the fat man. He was lying on his side, his hands secured behind him, and as he and Steve talked, Santa let out the most raunchy, stinkiest fart he could force out of his large ass.

Like acid, the fart began to eat away at the rope securing Santa's hands, the foulness slowly corroding the twine that made up the rope. Santa could already feel the ropes loosening around his wrists, and his hands clenched into fists as he prepared to break free.

"What's the matter, asshole? Nothing to say now?" Steve asked through clenched teeth.

Slut ran over to the bed and got in front of Steve, her face only inches from Santa's. "How could you do that to the other elves? You made us 'eat' them for Christ's sake. Why? It's…it's inhuman."

Santa needed more time to let the ropes disintegrate from his wrists, so Slut's question was the perfect excuse to stall for time. Normally, he would never have bothered explaining himself, but now he did just that. "We were out of food, you all know that. I had no choice. It was either start eating the elves or starve to death once water wasn't enough to keep us going."

"Yeah, Santa," Happy said as he joined Slut by the bed, "but there were only a few of us elves left anyway. Sooner or later you would've been down to none. Then what would you do?"

Santa shrugged. "I wasn't thinking that far ahead. I hoped that if I could give Martha and myself more time, maybe something else would come along."

"Then why were you feeding us, too?" Slut asked.

Santa smiled grimly. "Why? Because the livestock needs to be fed, too, that's why. I needed to keep you all fat and healthy, so there would be some meat on your bones when your time came to go into the pot."

Steve gripped the meat cleaver harder. "You sick fuck, you'll pay for killing my brothers and sisters." He was about to move closer, and shove Slut and Happy out of the way so he could kill Santa and end this once and for all, when the fat man suddenly swung his arms around, now free of their bindings, and placed his meaty palms on Slut's right cheek and Happy's left one. Like he was clapping symbols, he slammed their heads together so hard that both the elves' heads seemed to implode, much like a ripe pumpkin would do if dropped from a tall height.

As the small bodies slid to the floor like two ragdolls, Santa roared in anger and jumped out of the bed. Handsome Joe was just standing there, staring at the carnage before him. He got in Santa's way and the fat man backhanded the terrified elf, sending Handsome Joe flying across the room. He bounced off the wall, landed on a small sofa, and rolled onto the floor. Steve watched it all happen like it was in slow motion, and he also saw Handsome Joe remain still after landing. Whether the elf was alive or dead was unknown.

Steve knew he was alone now, either way. There would be no help in taking down the fat man.

"Come here, you little shit," Santa growled. "I'm gonna squeeze the life outta ya. Then I'm gonna take your lifeless corpse and the others and have a fucking feast that will keep me in meat for months to come."

"Fucking cannibal," Steve hissed as he backed away from Santa.

"I'm not a cannibal," Santa scoffed. "I'm human, and elves are something else altogether. If anyone here's a cannibal, it's you. I don't recall seeing you pushing your bowls of stew away, and in fact, I remember you licking your bowl clean each time."

"I didn't know!" Steve yelled and ran at Santa, the cleaver leading the way. Steve swung the cleaver back and forth, hoping the blurring weapon would be enough to keep Santa at bay.

But Santa had more than two feet of height on the short elf, and his arms gave him a greater reach. It was child's play to avoid the cleaver, then reach in and punch Steve in the face.

The elf went flying backwards, his feet backpedaling to try and keep him upright. But he tripped over Mrs. Claus body and fell right on his back.

Santa laughed when he saw his opponent go down. He trod across the bedroom, his footfalls shaking the lamp on the nightstand. He towered over Steve, and with a laugh of triumph, raised his right foot into the air, his aim to squash Steve under his heel. "I'm gonna flatten you like the piece of reindeer shit you are."

Steve could only lie there, staring up into Santa's evil face. He looked into the fat man's eyes, and saw only his death. There would be no mercy from the fabled St. Nick this night.

As the foot began to descend, Steve could do nothing but close his eyes and brace for what he prayed would be brief pain, before death took him.

But just as he expected the foot to come down, Santa began to yell in pain.

Steve opened his eyes to see Handsome Joe lying across from him, his teeth sunk deep into Santa's ankle, right around his Achilles' heel.

Santa began to wobble as the only leg supporting his massive girth began to buckle thanks to the severing of important tendons in his ankle. Handsome Joe, seeing Santa was about to come toppling down like a mighty redwood, rolled out of the way, spitting blood the entire time. The elf had come to just in time to save Steve, and his quick thinking had just saved Steve from a very messy death.

Santa couldn't fight gravity, and he dropped to the floor, landing so hard that the nightstand jumped two inches before falling back to the floor. Steve knew he'd been given a precious chance to win this battle, but he had to act fast, before Santa regained his wits.

Snapping up the cleaver that had fallen from his hands, he leaped over Mrs. Claus and onto Santa's belly. "Hey, Santa, do you know what day this is?"

Santa blinked, the question taking him off guard considering everything that was happening. "No, I uh, no I don't."

"It's ten minutes after midnight. So it's Christmas day." He raised the cleaver high and began bringing it down. "Merry fucking Christmas." The cleaver sank right between Santa's eyes, going in so deep that it stuck there. Steve couldn't get it out. Santa roared in anger and pain, and Steve was thrown off Santas' belly like the fat man was a bucking bronco.

Steve was thrown to the floor; he slid across it to hit the wall, his head taking the brunt of the impact. Dazed, the elf looked groggily up to see Santa rising on his knees, before coming to a standing position. He didn't use the leg Handsome Joe had bitten, but put all his weight on the good leg.

Steve couldn't believe what he was seeing. Santa was unstoppable; there truly was no beating this mythical behemoth.

Opening and closing his hands, Santa mimicked how he was going to crush Steve within them. "Now you die, little elf."

Steve could only look up at the towering giant before him. All he'd managed to do was buy himself a few more minutes of life.

Santa managed to take one step, then his bad ankle gave out and he plummeted to the floor like the same tree he'd mimicked only moments before. He tried to put his hands out to break his fall, but he wasn't thinking about the cleaver still embedded in his forehead. When he hit the floor belly first, he teetered forward like a weeble, and his head struck the floor hard. When this happened, the cleaver was forced even deeper into his head, this time severing something that mattered, and putting out the lights in Santa's eyes in the blink of an eye. By the time Santa was done weebling and wobbling, he was already dead.

Handsome Joe was the first to his feet, and he helped Steve to stand as well.

"Thanks, Joe, I owe you my life."

Handsome Joe just shrugged. His lips were still bright red with Santa's blood. "I'm just glad he's dead." He looked over at the corpses of Slut and Happy. "To bad they didn't make it."

Steve glanced at the two fallen elves. "Yeah, it sucks, as Happy would say."

Handsome Joe gestured to the corpses of Santa and his wife. "What should we do with them?"

Steve gave it some thought, but only briefly. "I think I have an idea. Will you give me a hand?"

"Of course."

The two elves got to work.

It was late evening when Handsome Joe joined Steve in the dining room. Steve had been left alone for the entire day, and Joe had been anxiously waiting to see what Steve was doing. His eyes went wide when he entered the dining room though. He said nothing, however, figuring Steve would explain the tableaux before him soon enough.

Steve was standing at the head of the table, where Santa had once sat. In his hand was a large carving knife, and all the seats had dishes and glasses before them. "For the others. They can be here in spirit at least," Steve said with a smile, then gestured for Handsome Joe to take a chair to the right of him. "Sit here, Joe."

Handsome Joe blinked. That was the second time Steve had called him 'Joe.' He said as much, too.

"I figure Joe is good enough seems it's just you and me now. No more nicknames, no more bullshit."

"I'd like that," Joe said with a wan smile.

"You hungry?" Steve asked.

"Starving actually," Joe replied.

"Then let's eat."

Before Steve and Joe, lying in the center of the table, was a naked and cooked Santa Claus. He'd been roasted like a pig over a fire for hours, and now his skin was burnt and flaking. There was an apple in his mouth as well, something Steve had found in the back of one of the cupboards, a lucky find if there ever was one. The cleaver was still in Santa's forehead. It had been jammed in there too hard to even try and take out, the skull seeming to clamp around it like a vise. Steve didn't mind. He leaned over the table after climbing onto the chair to get a good reach, and began sawing at Santa's belly.

"I'll take some from the upper leg, if you don't mind," Joe said.

"Huh? Oh sure, of course." Steve shifted position and began cutting some 'dark meat.'

"Steve, you are aware that by eating him we really will be cannibals," Joe said in a flat tone.

Steve shrugged as he slid the juicy meat onto Joe's plate. "Not according to Santa we aren't. He's human and we're elves. Different species."

"Oh, okay then, I'm too hungry to argue that much anyway."

In the corner of the dining room, the Christmas tree was lit up, the lights flickering red, yellow and blue, while outside, a gentle snow was falling.

Steve relished the first bite he had of Santa. It tasted of justice, and of revenge—both were the same in most ways.

The refrigerator was packed with pieces of Mrs. Claus and the other elves, and Santa alone was large enough to keep the two elves fed for months. And when the meat finally ran out, the two could set off for the mainland, to see how bad the zombie apocalypse truly was.

It might not have been a very Merry Christmas for the two elves, and in fact, it was something else altogether: more like a very dead Christmas.

Steve sank his teeth into the meat before him, chewing with gusto.

At that moment he decided it wasn't all bad, after all, he was still alive, and with Joe by his side, he wasn't alone.

The rest would work itself out.

You know, I just realized that there were absolutely no zombies in this story, which is kind of odd for a story that was supposed to mix Christmas with zombies.

"That's because you suck as a writer," Steve snapped, still sore over that 'short' jab he'd gotten back at the beginning of the story. "I've read better shit on the bathroom wall."

You know, Steve, you can really be a big dick.

"Maybe, but Big Dick is dead, so I guess it's okay."

Let's end this story, okay? I think we've said everything that needs to be said here.

"I couldn't agree more." Steve hesitated before adding, "Asshole."

Sigh.

Merry Christmas, everyone.

ONE MORE CHRISTMAS

The snow blew across the ice-crusted window, thanks to gusts of wind that swirled and spun the flakes in the air, as if they were trapped inside a cyclone.

Drifts lined the outer walls of the cabin, and the temperature had dropped to zero.

It was an angry day at the North Pole, in both weather and the mood of Santa Claus, who stood at the window, his arms crossed over his chest, his mouth set into a deep frown.

Despite the blowing snow, he could still see across the landscape to the small cemetery that contained the rest of the residents of the North Pole. The plot of land was situated on a hillside, and though there were no trees, it had a grand view of the setting sun each night.

Santa squinted as he peered out the window at the small grave markers. He knew exactly which one was for his late wife. Martha had died more than six months ago, after taking ill from a zombie bite, thanks to one of the infected elves.

One of the elves had snuck away from the North Pole, wanting to see if the zombie apocalypse was really true. About a hundred miles south was a small town hidden amongst the mountains. The plague that made the dead rise had traveled even to this small town, and before the naïve elf realized it, he had become surrounded by the walking dead. Well, being small and much faster than the shambling dead, he had managed to get back to his one-reindeer sleigh and escape before being eaten. But he hadn't escaped unscathed, and the bite on his palm was proof of it. Keeping his little jaunt to himself, it wasn't long before the elf died and reanimated, and then began to feed on the first elf he came upon.

Soon, the undead were filling the North Pole, and only Santa and Martha remained, the rest either torn apart or becoming zombies.

Then an undead elf managed to get inside the cabin Santa and his wife called home, and Martha was bitten before Santa could stomp the little bastard into paste, his large black boots flattening the elf until there was nothing remaining but a bloody gruel spreading across the floor.

Martha had taken three days to die, Santa holding a death vigil over her bed the entire time. When she finally passed on he had been there, a sharpened candy cane in his hand. The tip of the sharpened weapon had slid easily into her right ear, only the littlest bit of blood seeping out around the red and white instrument to pool on the pillowcase.

She was buried there, on that hillside, under the snow, the cold embrace of ice now her only lover.

Santa sighed heavily as he thought about the fate of the world. Just like Martha, he was immortal, but that only meant he had a life span that was forever as far as aging went. Suffering mortal harm, such as an infectious bite from the undead, well, that was a whole new ballgame. He could live forever only if he didn't suffer harm, and what the world now had was harm in abundance.

Leaving the window, he made himself a pot of hot chocolate, then went to the computer where he could search the internet, the pot of cocoa there to help him work his way through the hours. Each day he spent three to four hours surfing different message boards, hoping to see someone post or tweet, or send an e-mail to him or someone else.

The internet was still active, though no one was posting any-where anymore, and many sites were going down or becoming inactive with time. It was as if the entire thing was running on automatic.

It was hard to believe in a world of billions of people, that not one person was alive to send a message, but here he was, on yet another day, staring at the glowing screen, and praying for a miracle.

He thought back to years ago, before the internet, when he used to get bags full of letters, all addressed to Santa Claus, via the North Pole of course. But those days were long gone. The past few years, he got e-mails from children who told him what they wanted and how good they'd been that year. But near the end, when the last e-mails were still coming in, he got very different messages from children. The letters were terrifying, kids begging for Santa to help them, that their parents were zombies and were even now banging on their bedroom doors, as the parents tried to reach their children and feed.

He wrote back, trying to get the children to tell him where they were, and maybe he could try to rescue them. But each time Santa replied he received no response, and he feared the worst for each child.

That was over two years ago.

Over two years since the last contact with the outside world. Since then, all had been dark, not so much as a peep from someone somewhere.

By the time he finished off his pot of hot chocolate, Santa turned off the monitor and decided to call it a day. It was just as his hand was reaching for the switch to power down the screen that he heard a sound he never thought he would hear again.

A soft beep.

A beep that signified he had an e-mail.

He always kept his website—Santa.com—open but had it shrunk down to a hidden window in case he got a message. Frankly, he'd forgotten about it for months. But the window had been there, always open.

Opening the e-mail—the subject heading was from 'Timmy McCormick, age seven'—Santa's eyes went wide with surprise, shock, relief and then dread as he began to read the e-mail.

Dear Santa Claus,

I don't know if you're out there, or even still alive, but I have no one else to turn to.

Mommy and Daddy are dead.

I'm in the attic now, hiding. I've been here for more than a month. My family and I were living in a bomb shelter under the house, but when the food finally ran out, along with fuel for the tiny generator in the shelter, Daddy said we had no choice; we had to leave or starve to death.

The monsters have gotten into the house and I'm so scared. I know I should be brave, after all, I'm almost seven, but I can't help it.

When Mommy and Daddy made me come up here, Daddy gave me his laptop. He told me to hold on to it for him.

It was as I climbed into the attic that the monsters came up the stairs to the second floor.

Mommy screamed and Daddy turned to fight them. He told me to be brave, and not to come down no matter what I heard.

Daddy tried to get Mommy to climb the small, fold-down ladder to the attic with me but she wouldn't leave him. She said she would fight by his side. I could see the tears running down her cheeks as she said this.

That was when one of the monsters got by Daddy and grabbed Mommy.

I…I try not to think what Mommy looked like as the monster sank its teeth into her neck. I saw Mommy's eyes go wide with pain. But there was something else there, too. Something I don't really understand. It was sadness, I think, the sorrow of knowing she wouldn't get to see me again. That whatever happened next, she wouldn't be a part of it.

I'm pretty smart, huh, Santa? Mommy says I'm smarter than I should be for my age. I get all A's in school, too, or I did when there was a school. I haven't been to school in years now; I miss it a lot. All my friends, and the teachers. I guess they're all dead now.

Mommy managed to push the ladder closed, then she shoved it back up into the attic opening as she yelled for me to stay quiet. That was all I could do, I was so scared. I still am.

Just before the ladder closed and locked me in the attic, I saw Mommy and Daddy surrounded by those monsters, and then the monsters were eating them.

I sat in silence for hours, not moving, not breathing. I could hear the monsters down below, walking around, banging against the walls. The sounds of them feeding on my parents made me sick and I almost threw up once, but I remembered what Mommy said and I stayed quiet.

When I thought it was safe to move, I crawled to the fold-down ladder. There was a really thin line separating the trapdoor along the frame and I could see down to the floor. By looking through that line with one eye closed, I could see the hallway a little.

I saw Mommy and Daddy but they didn't look like I remembered them.

Mommy had only half a face and most of her scalp was missing. Daddy only had one arm, the missing one in the mouth of another monster. His stomach had been torn open and his insides were hanging out, swinging back and forth as he stumbled around the hallway. I stared at them for almost five minutes and finally I couldn't look anymore.

I cried then. I cried for Mommy and Daddy, and I cried for me, too. I was an orphan now. What was I supposed to do?

I sat there, silent, alone in the attic darkness for almost half a day when I realized the laptop was right there. I used it all the time in the shelter to play games so I couldn't believe I'd ignored it. I bet Daddy would have said it was shock I was feeling.

That's what I'm doing now, Santa, I'm e-mailing you to tell you that I don't know what to do. I need help, Santa. I have some food, all dried stuff that had been stored in the attic years ago, and there's a hole in the roof where I can collect rainwater, but I don't know how long I can last like this. I need you to come kill the bad monsters—Mommy and Daddy too now—and save me.

I've been a really good boy this year too, Santa. I always did what Mommy told me and I never talked back to Daddy.

I have to go to the bathroom, but other than a bucket in the corner left over from Mommy's gardening, I don't know what else to use. There are no windows up here so I can't see outside, but Daddy had gone to one of the boarded-up windows before he sent me to the attic and he told me that there's nothing left to see out there. That the neighborhood I live in is gone, that the houses on the street are mostly destroyed by fire. Only mine and the one next door on the left are still standing.

I'm so scared, Santa. I don't want to die, and though I'm smart, I'm still just a kid, and I really need you to come and find me.

The battery on the laptop is already low so I don't know how long it will stay on. It wasn't charged much when we left the shelter. Like I said before, once we ran out of fuel for the small generator, there was no power to charge it.

Please come save me.

> Timmy McCormick
> 1151 Melville Way
> Waterford, Ct 06385

Santa leaned back, the chair creaking softly. His eyes roamed over the e-mail once more as he thought about what he'd just read.

A child.

Alive.

When he thought there was no one left.

He stood up and walked back to the window, his gaze once more falling on the grave markers in the distance. He was alone here at the North Pole, and for a while he'd been wondering what he should do next.

But now his next move was clear, and when he considered it some more, he knew it was really the only thing to do.

He needed to go to Connecticut and find the boy, and save him from a fate worse than death.

Ironically, it was two months till Christmas, but until that exact moment, the date hadn't mattered. Santa scowled through his beard as he watched the falling snow.

It looked like there would be one more Christmas left in him, after all. He would save Timmy, and give the boy his life for a Christmas present, and together the two of them would live happily ever after.

But first he needed to prepare for the journey from the North Pole, through Canada, and then the United States. He knew it wouldn't be an easy one. He would be fighting the walking dead with each step he took.

But he was up for the job. He was Santa Claus, goddamn it.

He would make it to the boy and save him, even if it cost him his life in the process.

It took Santa half a day to prepare for the journey. Loaded with weapons and supplies, he hooked up the reindeer to his sleigh and got ready to leave.

He was down a few reindeer, the undead elves having got to them before Santa could save them. But the rest had been kept locked in the barn and so hadn't been ravaged by the undead dwarves.

Santa still wore his bright red suit, but it was now rather different from what it once was. Across his chest was a heavy bandolier, filled with hand grenades. On each one was written the word Ho, so that together it read Ho-Ho-Ho.

He'd done it at the last minute, liking the irony of it all.

On each hip was a twelve-inch candy cane, the thickness around more than an inch. It was the jumbo-sized ones he would leave with presents under trees of really good children. The tips of each candy cane had been filed down to a ruthless point, one that would stab or gouge out an eye with ease.

On his back, slung over casually, was an M-16A rifle.

Sure, he was Santa Claus, but even he needed to defend himself against the walking dead, and a rifle would do the job better than anything else he could think of. In the back of the sleigh was a large bag, but it wasn't filled with toys, oh no. Now it was filled with anything Santa could think of that might be of use fighting off the undead as he made his way to Connecticut.

The sleigh itself was also fortified, steel plates surrounding the sleigh on both sides. It was light-weight metal, but it would do the job of fending off hands and teeth that would be trying to reach him.

"Okay, boys, it's time to leave," he said to the reindeer, who all snorted in reply like horses. Their breath fogged before them, filling the air with moisture. Their bodies were wrapped with leather to help protect them from attackers.

He thought about Timmy, who didn't even know Santa was coming. He'd tried to contact the boy but there had been no reply. But the kid had said the laptop battery was low, so he hoped that was the reason for no reply.

"Yeaah!" he yelled, shaking the reins to get the lead reindeer moving. "Onward, my friends! Take me to Timmy!"

The snow-covered ground began to shake as the reindeer began to gallop, pulling the sleigh out onto the frozen tundra. Then, with a mighty heave, the two lead reindeer leapt into the air, the others following. The sleigh seemed to hang back for just a second, as if it knew it wasn't supposed to leave the ground, but then it gave in and was soaring through the air.

The cold wind whipped Santa's beard wildly, and his nose and cheeks immediately became red. That was where he got such rosy cheeks, from the wind hitting him as he flew through the air. It wasn't because he was jolly; it was because he was in the first stages of frostbite. But being immortal, he always healed quickly

As he reached the clouds, Santa had to admit he felt lighter in his heart. It was as if all the loss, grief and sorrow were being left behind at the North Pole. In fact, as he gazed down at the ground, which was already lost from sight due to his altitude, he wondered if he would ever return to the place.

For what had once been a place of joy and cheer was now nothing but echoes of laughter, of faded dreams and a life now finished. Whatever he had there with his wife was over, and there was nothing that would ever change that.

Maybe it was a good thing; this odyssey to save one small boy. For Santa quickly realized his existence at the North Pole was meaningless.

Without children to love him, to pray to him on Christmas Day for presents, he truly was nothing. His purpose, one he'd had for hundreds of years, was over, and nothing in the world could ever change that outcome.

But now, as he stared out onto the horizon, the clouds surrounding him like white fog, he felt energized.

He had a purpose again.

It was as he flew over Boston that the shit hit the fan, as the saying goes.

It was night as he soared over downtown, and just as he was over the Financial District, he began to take gunfire.

The moon was out, and its pale glow illuminated the entire scene to Santa, though later, he wished he could wipe the images from his mind.

He was staring idly out across the dark horizon, the undulating heads of the reindeer lulling him into relaxation, when suddenly the two lead reindeer's heads just disappeared, as if something had reached down from the heavens and popped the heads like they were annoying zits on a giant face.

He only had time to blink in surprise as he tried to take in what he'd just witnessed, his mind trying to accept if it was true or perhaps he had dozed off and was dreaming. But then the wind took the blood, brains and bone matter and blew it into his face, the bone like shrapnel, which peppered his cheeks as if he'd flown into a hailstorm.

A split-second after that came the sound of what reminded him of sporadic gunfire, and as he peered down over the side of the sleigh, he spotted the wink-wink of what had to be the gunfire's origin coming from one of the closest rooftops.

Then two more reindeer were hit in their torsos, and their screams of pain and terror filled the night. Santa barely had time to grip the front of the sleigh before it began to fall, as the rest of the reindeer were riddled with automatic gunfire.

70mm bullets tore the animals' bodies to shreds in seconds, and Santa could only watch helplessly as his loyal steeds were reduced to nothing but bloody meat.

Then with no flying reindeer left to pull the sleigh through the air, he found himself dropping like a lead weight, as bloody pieces of reindeer flew all around him.

He was struck hard in the face with something wet and furry, but as to what piece it was or what reindeer it belonged to, he would never know.

His stomach lurched as he plummeted to the ground, as if he was on a lurching elevator. Looking below him, the earth was approaching far too fast for his liking. He didn't panic, however, his mind already formulating a plan to save himself.

He wasn't close to any rooftops, so he acted fast, and pushing off the sleigh with his boots, he jumped into the air and to the side. The sleigh was forced away from him, to begin spinning, the pieces of reindeer still tangled in the reins flapping every which way.

He shifted his body so that he began to angle towards a rooftop, his large girth working well for him, his body a giant sail.

His beard flapped up and over his face, blinding him at times, but there was no time to even try to get it off his face and eyes.

The rooftop was coming far too fast for his liking but there were no other options.

The sleigh was slightly below him and he heard the crash when it struck the edge of the roof before he saw it. Splintering into hundreds of pieces of wood, the sleigh shattered upon impact, then tumbled over the side to fall to the dark street below. Santa knew his body would have been mixed in with that mess if he hadn't jumped clear of the sleigh.

But then there was no time for thought, as the rooftop came up and under him. He did his best to roll, trying to absorb the kinetic energy of the fall, but still his body took a pounding.

The rifle slung across his shoulder dug into his back, and he let out a howl of pain from the shock. The rooftop was covered in gravel, and this provided a much-needed cushion for his body. Still, shards of rock came up and struck his face, cutting and slicing his skin. He rolled ass over elbows, crossing the entire length of the rooftop in seconds. As he tumbled, he glimpsed the edge of the roof, and saw it getting closer with each tumble. He was going to go right over the side if he didn't do something fast.

Once more time stood still, and before he could figure out something, he was hitting the one-foot-high lip of the rooftop and flipping right over it. His gloved hand slapped out into the air, hoping to grab something, anything to halt his fall to the street below. He felt himself going over, and then, when he should have kept going down, he was lurched backwards to hang there against the wall. It was as if a giant hand had grabbed him and pulled him back like he had been a dog on its owner's leash getting a pull-back.

He sucked in a lungful of air as he blinked in surprise. He was hanging there, and when he looked down past his boots, he could see the distinct shape of figures shuffling about on the ground.

It took almost a full minute for Santa to gather himself enough to realize he was caught on a protuberance on the rooftop lip—the strap to his M16A had become caught, and the fortunate occurrence had saved his fat ass from a fate worse than death.

He let out a hearty "Ho-ho-ho" as he accepted the luck that had been thrown his way by whatever cosmic force ruled the universe, then he carefully maneuvered his body to a better position and climbed back onto the rooftop. When he fell the few inches to the roof, feeling the solid ground beneath him, he let out a heavy sigh of relief. Whatever came next was an unknown, but at least for this second in time he was alive and safe.

As he laid there, his eyes closed, relishing the moment, he heard the distinct sound of feet crunching on gravel.

He slowly turned his head, not really thinking about what he might see.

Five figures were closing toward him, and by the way they moved, they were humans, not zombies. Four were men, and one was a woman, but by the haircut, cut of her jawline and clothes, she looked more masculine than some of the men.

The man in the lead was smiling widely, the machete in his right hand covered in a dark brown substance that had to be dried blood. "Well, well, will you look at what we got here. If it isn't Santa Claus." His eyes gleamed with malevolence, and when he smiled, the clear tips of his filed and pointed teeth could be seen.

He glanced over his shoulder at his companions, his next words more for them than Santa. "Hey, guys, it looks like we're gonna get to eat somethin' exotic tonight."

Santa was pulled to his knees roughly by two of the strangers, both men holding him roughly, their grips like steel vices. The woman took the M16 and his bandolier full of grenades from him, then stepped back two feet, as if she wanted to stay close to him.

"You don't seem surprised to see me," Santa said. "Most people would think I'm a mall Santa or something. They sure as hell wouldn't believe I'm real."

The lead man let out a sharp bark of laughter. "Shit, man, have you seen the world? The dead are fucking walkin'. You see shit like that and Santa Claus in a magic sleigh with a bunch of fucking reindeer don't seem like such a wide stretch." He shrugged. "Guess you could say the whole zombie apocalypse thing has opened our minds to other possibilities."

"And then some," one of the men said, as he took in Santa's wide girth. "Fuck, Troy, this guy's gonna feed us for a month."

"Hell yeah he is," Troy replied as he raised the machete high over his head.

Santa glared at Troy, then the others as well. "You know, boys and girls, Santa knows when you've been naughty or nice, and from the looks of you five, I'm putting you all on the naughty list right now."

"Like I give a shit," Troy said as the machete began to come down right at Santa's head.

But Santa hadn't been standing idle, he'd been taking in the scene before him, figuring out a plan of action. As Troy came at him with the machete, the two men holding Santa lessened their grip in expectation of the chop that would split Santa's skull in twain.

Santa was ready for this, and the instant the hands on him loosened, he shrugged the men off by bringing his arms straight up, and then reached down and pulled a candy cane from each hip, bringing them up point first.

The first candy cane was thrown like a dagger, the tip going straight into Troy's right eye. The man had time for a brief scream of shock and pain before the tip pierced his brain, killing him instantly. He was still moving forward though, the machete already coming down, and Santa shifted his weight and threw one of the men that had been holding him at Troy.

The machete struck the man in the shoulder, slicing deep. The man howled in agony as blood geysered from the wound. Troy fell on top of the screaming man, nothing but a dead weight, and the man became trapped. He howled some more as he tried to escape the body pinning him, while the entire time his life's blood squirted out of his open wound.

Santa wasn't staying still while this happened, and he spun to the left, using the second candy cane to stab the other man who had been holding him in the chest. The tip of the candy cane went deep, and though it missed the man's heart, it did enough damage to put the guy out of action.

The woman was fumbling with the M16A she was holding, but Santa was on her in a flash. He punched her in the face, grabbed the rifle from her hands, and spun it around to shoot her in the face. The back of her head exploded, taking most of her brains with it.

There was one man left, and he stood stock still, the violent actions before him taking him completely off guard. Santa spun around, expecting to be attacked, but the man just looked at Santa with wide eyes.

"Oh shit, what the fuck just happened?" the man stammered.

Santa leveled the rifle at the man and squeezed the trigger, but just before he did, he replied, "Simple. You lost the fight." Then the man was sprayed with half a dozen bullets, as the rifle fired on semi-auto. The body was thrown backwards from the force of the bullets, and it fell off the edge of the roof. Santa heard it hit bottom, the meaty splat undeniable.

Shaking his head, Santa tsked, tsked. "Very naughty indeed."

He gathered what weapons he could from the bodies, and retrieved his bandolier of grenades and candy cane weapons as well, wiping the blood off the candy daggers on the clothes of the corpses. He went through the pockets of the bodies as well, but found little he wanted. One had been holding a small sack of what looked like beef jerky, but on closer examination, a piece of jerky had what sure looked like a tattoo of a butterfly, though it was faded and hard to make out, as the meat had been dried and the art was wrinkly. He tossed the bag to the side, not wanting it.

When he had all he could use, he moved out, a slight limp to his gait from his fall onto the roof. But he healed fast, and by the time he was halfway down the stairwell that led to the street, his limp was almost gone.

"Looks like I'm on foot for now," he said under his breath. He glanced up at the ceiling of the stairwell, his mind going back to the four corpses up there. "Assholes. Thanks for nothing."

When he reached the bottom floor of the building, he kicked open a door leading out to the street, then moved into the shadows to continue his journey.

The first half of the new leg of the journey was hard. Being on foot, he was vulnerable to attack. Zombies came from all directions, stumbling and shambling, all trying to reach him.

Santa used the urban landscape to stay one step ahead of the walking dead. Climbing over rubble and climbing onto abandoned vehicles. The zombies weren't as agile and were quickly left behind. When Santa ran out of obstacles to avoid the dead, he had to fight. His M16A spit fire again and again, shooting the zombies and stopping them in their tracks.

Stopping at a hospital, he regrouped inside the foyer leading into the emergency room. To his right an ambulance had gone through the wall, cement and rubble covering its hood. At first Santa barely paid it any attention, but as he rested, he decided to investigate.

The keys were still in the ignition, the engine off, as was the electrical. A headless corpse was behind the steering wheel, the visible arms shriveled, the skin dry.

Grabbing the corpse, he pulled it free of the seat and tossed it to the side. When the body landed, a puff of dust came from it.

He didn't know why he bothered, but for the hell of it Santa turned the key in the ignition. At first there was a dry click, but a moment later the starter began to crank a bit. It was a weak showing but still, at least there was power. Santa turned the ignition off and sat for a moment, then with a silent prayer, turned the key again. Once more the starter cranked, and then suddenly, the engine sputtered and came to life.

A large belch of smoke shot from the exhaust and there was a loud pop. But the engine was running, even if it was more of a sputter. Carefully, Santa gave the engine some gas and the idle evened out, and as the choke kicked in the motor began to run more steadily.

A sound of shifting rubble came from the driver's side, as Santa sat with the door hanging open; he barely heard it over the rumbling engine.

He was just turning his head to look in the direction of the noise when two zombies seemed to pop up out of thin air, their hands grabbing him, teeth snapping at his exposed face.

And just like that, Santa was in a fight for his life.

One hand got tangled in Santa's beard, and he yelped in pain as the zombie tugged. The other one was trying to bite off an ear. The ghoul was a fat one, and nearly as large as Santa.

Bringing up the machete he'd taken from the fallen cannibal leader, Santa slashed down before him. The pressure yanking on his beard lessened and the zombie fell back. But the fat one trying to eat his ear was still aggressively attacking, and Santa kicked out with a large black boot to stop it. But the boot only grazed the side of the zombie and the ghoul came at him even faster than before, seeing that it had an opening. Santa leaned into the ambulance some more to get some room, and though awkward, managed a clumsy sideways slash at the obese zombie.

The blade was sharp, and the tip sank two inches into the zombie's huge stomach, leaving a long, open wound. There was a squelching sound, similar to a bucket of organs at a butcher shop being dumped onto the floor; a wet splashing sound that would make a man squeamish, no matter how hard his constitution.

The noise came from the fat zombie.

With its gut sliced open like a landed fish being prepared for dinner, entrails by the yards began to pour out, splashing onto the ground, the greasy ropes becoming entangled in the zombie's feet to trip it up.

The odor of rotting meat and excrement filled the air, and Santa gagged from the smell. Bile rose in his throat and it was all he could do to keep it down.

The first zombie that had been shoved away began to crawl across the ground, then stopped at the sprawling intestines. With one grubby hand it scooped up a few ropes, and began to shove them into its mouth. The ropes squirted and burst from the pressure as teeth tore into the meaty tendrils.

That was too much for Santa, and he leaned back onto the passenger seat of the ambulance and vomited the contents of his stomach onto the floorboards.

The fat zombie with its gut ripped open tried to reach Santa, and with the pressure of the zombie on the ground holding it back by the intestines, even more were pulled out. Row after row of greasy ropes spilled out of the huge gut, a gore-inspired magician's magic scarf trick taken to an entirely new level.

But the ropes were long, almost infinite, and the fat zombie still managed to reach Santa.

Disgusted like he'd never been, Santa pulled a leg up to his chin as much as he was able given his girth, and kicked out with his foot. The large black sole of his boot connected squarely with the zombie's chubby face, crushing its nose and sending shards of cartilage and bone into its brain, killing it almost instantly.

It dropped to the ground, still twitching as whatever foul life inhabited it shrank away, while the other zombie still fed on what it managed to grab.

Santa pushed off the seat and got free of the ambulance, then walked the few feet separating him and the feeding zombie. Raising the machete, he slashed at the neck of the ghoul, but though the blow was powerful, the head was only partially severed. Santa frowned, thinking how it wasn't at all like in the movies, where the hero swiped at the zombie and in one blow took off its head. No, in real life it was far more difficult; after all, he needed to carve through tendons, muscle and the spine to get the job done.

The head was lolling to one side as the zombie got to its feet. It was unsteady on its legs however, as its world view had shifted slightly thanks to a head not fully on its shoulders. It charged at Santa but missed him by three feet, moving right past him only to trip and fall to the ground.

It was almost comical.

Half-chewed intestines spilled back out from the severed esophagus, boiling forth like a volcano from the jagged neck wound. Santa didn't give the zombie a chance to get up. Moving on top of it, he stomped on its back with his left boot, trapping the body to the ground. Then he chopped at the neck again, and this time, with the job already half-done, the blade cleaved through the remaining mass of muscle and tendons to severe the head cleanly from the body, the blade then ricocheting off the stone covering the ground. The head rolled a few feet to the side, the mouth still chewing, the eyes sliding back and forth, as if the head was watching a tennis match.

Santa ignored the head; the threat was nullified. He felt something weighing slightly on his beard and he looked down to see that a severed hand was tangled in his beard. Disgusted, he pulled at it then let out a yelp when he felt pain in his chin. The damn thing was in there good. After wiping the machete clean on the clothes of the headless corpse, he cut the long white hairs wrapped around the hand. When he was done, there was the distinct impression of where he'd cut. He couldn't see it though, not unless he used a mirror. He threw the hand away, and with one last look around, returned to the ambulance.

The motor was still ticking away softly.

A low moan from behind made him turn to see a dozen more zombies approaching. Not wanting to deal with them as well, he climbed into the ambulance, slammed the driver's door closed, and backed the vehicle out of the hole in the wall. Rubble and debris rained down, some pattering on the hood before sliding off in clouds of dust. The windshield had a large crack across the middle but was still intact, which was good—it was still strong enough to provide protection if needed.

When he was free of the building, he spun the steering wheel to the right, and as the first zombie slapped the back of the vehicle with its pale hands, he stepped on the gas pedal and began to move forward.

Glancing in the cracked side mirror, Santa watched the zombies recede.

The gas gauge on the dashboard indicated there was a quarter tank of fuel left. Not much, and not enough to reach his destination, but one thing at a time. For now he had transportation and was moving once more.

It wasn't a flying sleigh, but it would get him where he needed to go.

Santa slowed his jog to more of a walk, as he tried to catch his breath.

It had been more than a week since he'd found the ambulance.

Used to flying in his sleigh, he had no conception of what it was like driving on the ground. He had barely managed to get five blocks from where he found the ambulance before the roads became impassible and the vehicle had to be abandoned.

But that wasn't the worst of his problems.

More and more zombies had seen him, and he'd been fighting for his life for each foot he made out of the city.

Once he had even tried to hide out in a decrepit apartment building, hoping the zombies would go away. But they never did, and worse, their constant moaning and pounding of fists on the windows and doors of the first floor of the building attracted even more.

To escape from that perilous predicament, he'd jumped from one building to the next, crashing through the fifth floor window of the adjacent building like some kind of action hero from a movie.

But it had worked and the zombies, concentrating on the building they believed he was in, had been completely oblivious that the prey had escaped.

But no sooner had Santa rounded the corner to continue his journey, then another half-dozen ghouls had seen him and begun to follow. And so the chase began anew, with almost similar results.

Eventually he did manage to leave Boston behind, and made his way up Rte 93 South. Then he'd gone onto 95 South and made his way to Connecticut. But the zombies were still following, a massive horde that he couldn't shake no matter how hard he tried.

His only good fortune was that he had managed to stay ahead of them, but with each passing hour, the horde was getting closer.

It was snowing, too. More than three inches an hour by his calculations. It made the going rough, as there was more than a foot on the ground now with the storm still going strong. At least it slowed the undead down as well and in fact, they seemed to be having a tougher time than he was.

Pausing for the briefest of moments, Santa leaned his head back and spread his lips wide to let snow fall into his mouth. He needed water and this was a simple fix. He glanced over his shoulder to see the horde was still there, just on the edge of visibility due to the storm.

They were a persistent bunch; he had to give them that.

Knowing he had to keep moving, he began to jog again, his breath puffing out before him as if he was a locomotive.

He was tired, so tired, but he wouldn't stop until he reached Timmy and saved the boy.

Then everything would be all right.

It had to be.

When Santa reached the Rhode Island border on Interstate 95, things grew worse—if that was even possible.

Not seeing a large pothole on the side of the road where he was jogging, he tripped in it, turning an ankle at the same time. Though the ankle would heal on its own soon enough, with the horde still on his tail, now was not the time to slow down, even for the amount of time it would take for him to heal.

The horde was so close he could hear them moaning, and their feet crunching in the ice-crusted snow. It was below freezing, though that didn't bother Santa in the least, and in fact, it re-minded him of home back at the North Pole.

He kept going, only now he was barely moving faster than walking speed. The snow was coming down harder as well, and it had the looks of a full-blown blizzard.

Shapes appeared before him, and before he knew what they were, seven zombies seemed to materialize as if by magic, thanks to the poor visibility.

Santa unslung the M16A from across his shoulder and shot all seven, one at a time. Bullets stitched up torsos to strike heads, exploding skulls in glorious sprays of red. The snow was painted crimson for a few brief sections before fresh-falling snow buried it. Santa never hesitated as he limped past the fallen corpses, using the guardrail to navigate by, as the road was all but invisible.

One zombie was still animated, though its lower spine had been severed by a bullet. It lay on the ground, half-buried in snow, its arms reaching for Santa as the large man went past it. Gnarled fingers grazed his black boots, but Santa didn't slow down nor move around the fallen ghoul. The ghoul wasn't dead but it was out of action; it was good enough for Santa.

His stomach growled and he cursed his luck. He'd run out of food a day ago, after having some of his supplies lost when he was running for his life. Ignoring the gnawing feeling in his gut, he trudged forward, wincing each time his turned ankle connected with the ground.

Santa almost let out a cry of relief when he spotted the green sign proclaiming **Welcome to Connecticut** emblazed in white.

With the wind flapping the edges of the rest stop map he had salvaged from an abandoned car's glove box, Santa quickly did a quick guess on how many miles he still needed to travel.

Too many, but still, he was on the last leg of his journey. Behind him, the zombies howled in frustration, still unable to catch him.

The horde was closer, too, less than three hundred feet. But an inch or a mile, it was irrelevant. They weren't close enough to attack him—that was all that mattered.

The snow had stopped falling, but the wind still blew in gusts that made snowdrifts everywhere, the flying snow blinding him.

But what hindered him did the same to the undead, so Santa took heart in that, at least. He considered going off the highway, to try and lead the horde away from him, then he could backtrack onto the highway and continue his quest in peace, but it would take hours off his journey, and in the end he decided not to bother.

Besides, Santa figured once he left the highway upon reaching Waterford, he could lose the horde then. Food had become a serious problem as well. A few times he'd come across cars on the side of the highway, and with some quick scavenging had managed to turn up some candy bars. One car had a half-eaten power bar stuck to the floorboards. Santa didn't care, he wasn't fussy at this point, and he ate the bar with gusto as he walked. Water wasn't a problem of course. All he had to do was scoop a handful and eat it, the fresh-fallen snow chilling his mouth as it melted.

The last car had almost been his undoing, though. A Honda Civic was parked at an odd angle, the front bumper touching the guardrail. It had been entirely covered in snow, and Santa hadn't been as cautious as he should have been upon investigating the vehicle due to his haste to keep moving.

He had just gone over to the driver's door and opened it, not bothering to clear a window off to peer inside. The instant he'd opened the door, a zombie had lunged out, though it was more of a clumsy fall than an actual jump. Having been trapped in the car, the zombie had been eager to escape its prison. Santa had staggered backwards, caught completely off guard as the zombie tumbled forth from the car to sprawl face-first into the snow.

Recovering quickly, Santa had used a candy cane dagger to stab the zombie in the right ear, jamming the spike deep into its brain. The body had shivered once, as if cold, and gone still. Santa had tried to pull the candy cane out but it had been stuck, and though he yanked with all his might, the damn thing was jammed in there good. Placing a boot on the back of the zombie's neck, he'd tried one more time, and this time had pulled so hard it came free, only he was thrown backwards to fall onto the snow. He'd laid there for a few brief seconds, looking up at the cloud-covered sky, then rolled to his knees and stood up.

The tip of the candy dagger had broken off in the skull of the zombie. The candy cane was useless now as a weapon so he'd tossed it away. Where it landed was unknown, as it sank into the snow and disappeared. He still had the other one at least.

Returning to the car, he'd ignored the odor of rotting meat. It wasn't that strong thanks to the cold, but it still tickled the back of his throat.

The vehicle had been devoid of anything useful; all that trouble for nothing.

Moaning drifted on the wind and Santa had looked behind him. The zombies were getting closer. He knew he needed to get moving, to keep the distance between them and him.

Stepping over the corpse, he'd continued onward.

By the time Santa reached the exit for Waterford, his ankle was long healed. He glanced over his shoulder as he began walking down the exit. The horde was still there, following him. He knew they would never stop; not unless they caught him or he somehow got away from them. It had been wishful thinking on his part that he could shake them on foot. If he'd managed to find transportation on the long walk to Waterford, then sure, he would have left the horde in his wake, but only being able to go as fast as a jog, well, he had never stood a chance.

So he was going to have to deal with them, as he didn't want to bring the horde to little Timmy's front door. He would have to find a spot to stand and fight, but he wanted to wait a little longer, just in case he got lucky and managed to lose them after all.

When he was close—but not too close—to Timmy's location, he would deal with the horde once and for all. He knew he would use up most of his resources when he fought, and he hated to waste his meager supplies of ammunition and grenades in such a wasteful way. But if it was the difference of destroying them now or having to fight past them later with Timmy in tow, then it was clear that sooner would be the appropriate time, rather than later.

It took him another three days to find Timmy's address, and by then Santa was running on fumes. He was exhausted, both mentally and physically.

The home had once been very nice. Santa imagined easily what it had looked like before the dead began to walk. A manicured lawn, two cars in the driveway, perhaps Timmy's bike lying on the grass of the front yard. The boy had been told countless times by his mother not to leave it there, but as children were wont to do, the kid never listened.

The first floor had a picture window dead center of the house, and Santa imagined a cat or small dog sitting there, sunning itself, the curtains fluttering lazily in the cool summer air.

He blinked, and in that instant, in his mind's eye the picture of the home was shattered, to be replaced with what was the reality of the home now.

All the windows were shattered, the glass shards remaining in the frames glistening in the sun like the icicles hanging from the gutters. The roof had shingles missing, and near the chimney it looked like a hole had formed. Santa thought that was good actually. It would have allowed the boy access to snow and rainwater as a water source.

In the picture window at the front of the house, all the panes shattered, could be seen the desiccated carcass of a cat or dog. It was nothing more than bones and skin, and what breed or what sort of animal it could have been was impossible to discern from where he stood.

A few zombies were moving in and out of the front door, which hung on one hinge. When they spotted Santa they started to move towards him.

"Timmy, if you can hear me!" Santa shouted at the house. "I'm here to rescue you, but first I need to take care of some unwanted company. I'll be back soon. Stay strong, son!"

He began to jog again, away from the house, but now he made sure the following horde was still with him.

Of course it was.

Just as he began to move, the first of the horde rounded the corner at the far end of the street. Santa made sure to stay in the center of the road to remain visible, not wanting his pursuers to lose him. It was finally the time of reckoning, and he would make sure enough of the horde was destroyed that they would not be a threat to him when he took the boy away from his home.

As he jogged down the street, his boots crunched in the snow, the sound deafening amongst the quiet ruins of the neighborhood.

The noise drew more zombies from their hiding places inside destroyed homes—mostly from fire. They stumbled out into the snow, some falling when they couldn't navigate the uneven ground. But they didn't feel the cold and so crawled until they could regain their footing.

Santa traveled an entire city block before spotting of all things, a red sleigh like the one he used to deliver presents. It was perched on a pedestal on a front lawn of a home long destroyed by fire.

Plastic reindeer, mostly buried under the snow, lay on their sides before the sleigh, and fake plastic presents sat in the back of it.

There was even a life-size Santa Claus sitting in the seat, the red suit faded and torn in places from exposure to the elements.

Santa jogged to the sleigh and jumped onto it, then kicked the fake Santa off with his right boot. The fake Santa's head went flying away to land in the snow, while the body tumbled heavily to land upside down.

Santa began to ready himself for the approaching horde. He had a few feet of height on them as he stood in the sleigh, but he knew he still needed to act fast and take them out quickly as he could.

They were only a hundred feet away and closing fast, when he took the first grenade from his bandolier and pulled the pin, his arm going far behind him to throw it.

"Merry Christmas, you undead bastards," he sneered, and after waiting for the count of three to let them get closer, he threw the grenade as hard as he could.

The small orb shot through the air to land twenty feet before the beginning of the horde, but Santa knew this would happen. With mostly ice and hard-packed snow on the ground, the grenade began to bounce and slide straight at the approaching dead. Like a hockey puck sliding on ice towards the goal, the grenade kept on moving, and only stopped when it struck the feet of a zombie. The zombie was female, but as to her age it was unknown, given her skin was sagging from decay, her eyes milky-white, her hair falling out in thick chunks along with her scalp. One breast was missing, the blouse hanging from her form in tatters. The blue slacks she had on were little more than rags, stained with a myriad of fluids, which were either dried or become frozen on the material.

She looked down when the grenade struck her feet, her head cocking to one side, as if she was a dog spotting something of interest. Bending over, the rest of the horde moving around her, she picked up the grenade and studied it, looking for all purposes like she was wondering if the small orb was edible.

When it exploded, she was vaporized, the shockwave sending any zombie within ten feet of her flying away, mostly in pieces.

Santa watched the explosion, and grinned beneath his beard as body parts began to rain down on the street, the cold meat slapping the snow and ice. He threw another grenade, this one landing in the center of the thick mob of bodies. When it exploded, arms and heads went flying in all directions, to then patter down onto the snow in thick chunks of flesh. With a snarl, Santa unslung his M16A and began to fire at the distracted zombies.

Jumping down off the sleigh, he moved into the crowd, for the moment barely noticed by them as they dealt with the shockwave from the grenades. Most zombies seemed confused, and only a few tried to attack him. He shot them down easily, and when he came upon one already down but not dead, he swung the machete high, slicing off its head or cleaving its skull like a madman on a killing spree.

A zombie snuck up behind him when Santa was busy dispatching a trio on the ground. The hand holding the machete was quickly grappled and he couldn't use it to get rid of the attacker. Taking the barrel of the rifle and swinging it around, he stuck it under his arm so that from behind, the barrel was peeking out from between his arm and the side of his body.

At waist level with the zombie grabbing him, he fired off a three-round burst that split the zombie in two, severing its spine easily.

The bottom part fell over, its insides splashing to stain the snow red, while the upper part tried to hang on to Santa's arm. He swung his arm around and the momentum sent the zombie flying away. As if he was skeet shooting, Santa shot the flying torso in midair, blowing apart the head and destroying the right shoulder.

The rear of the horde had been untouched by the grenades, so Santa sheathed the machete and readied another one. Pulling the pin with his teeth, he threw the grenade into the undead crowd, but was bumped by a zombie, his aim getting messed up. "Happy Hanukah, you assholes!" he yelled. But as soon as he threw the grenade he realized it was going to land a little too close for comfort.

"Come here, you," he said to a zombie, and pulled the body towards him to use as a shield. The grenade exploded a second later, and even through the zombie he held he could feel the shockwave and feel the impact of body parts hitting him.

After a few seconds he dropped the zombie to the ground. It rolled onto its back, and when Santa glanced at it, he saw that its entire front was nothing but shredded meat, a femur sticking out of its chest like a thrown dagger. The thing still moved slightly, twitching. Its face was gone, a mass of muscle, meat and tendons. Using his boot, Santa stomped on the ghoul's face, crushing the skull beneath his heel. Then the body was forgotten, and he pulled the machete free to begin the killing anew

"For Timmy!" he yelled as he waded into the horde, dealing death with every bullet fired from the rifle, and with each blow given from the machete.

When he was finally done and the M16A was out of bullets, nothing stirred on the street, with the exception of where rotting organs slid down the sides of snow-covered cars and other objects scattered around the street, such as a mailbox and a small newspaper kiosk.

The once pristine white of the area from the fallen snow was gone, to be replaced by the browns, purples and the dark reds of excrement and gore from over a hundred destroyed human bodies.

Nearby was a fallen zombie with no face, the features caved in by Santa's boot. Brains slid out of the open cavity, as well as mucus and other vicious fluids. Both eyes were pulped into mush, and they slid down the face to dribble onto the snow like spent pudding.

Satisfied with the destruction he'd wrought, Santa began walking back down the street towards Timmy's house. A few undead stragglers came at him, but it was a simple task to kill them.

When he reached Timmy's home, he entered through the open front door, and was greeted by a trio of zombies. One had two broken legs and crawled across the floor, while the other two came at him simultaneously.

He shoulder-checked one into the wall, the force of the hit so powerful that the zombie pretty much broke apart on impact. It left a dark stain on the plaster, which was cracked and dented from being struck. Santa punched the other zombie in the face. The white gloves he always wore were already stained brown and red from punching other zombies, so the added ichor was nothing to him. The punch was so hard that his fist sank up to the wrist in the zombie's face. When he withdrew it, there was a sucking sound, a squishy, wet noise that filled the house for a few seconds.

Shaking his hand to get off most of the gunk, he looked down to see the crawling zombie had reached him, its hands even now wrapping around his right boot, its teeth spread wide to try and bite him.

Disgusted, he kicked it away. The zombie spun in the air, flipping around, and landed on its head. There was a dull snap as its neck was broken. The half-corpse flopped around on the floor, its spine severed, immobile and harmless unless someone was stupid enough to walk up to it and shove an appendage into its clacking teeth.

After making sure there were no more threats, he moved up the stairs to the second floor, where the trap door to the attic should be.

Family photos lined the walls, the faces of smiling parents and a young boy of about six. Most of the pictures had been taken at Disneyland; a family vacation by the looks of it. He paused halfway up the stairs, studying the pictures. The people in the photos seemed so happy, so carefree.

Back when the picture was taken, who would have imagined the world would be what it was now? Probably no one. Certainly not him either. He'd lost everyone he'd ever loved: his wife, the elves, hell, even the reindeer were gone. All that he was, who he had become; it was all nothing but ash blowing in the wind.

A shuffling sound pulled him away from his reverie, and Santa climbed the remaining steps and stopped at the top landing.

There were two more zombies there, and both turned to face him as he stood before them, his right boot pressed on a piece of hardwood that creaked enough to alert the ghouls to his presence.

One was male, the other female. Santa studied them, and though decayed, their skin sagging, eyes withdrawn into their heads, lips pulled back and parts of their faces missing in places, he could still see the resemblance to the two adults in the family photos.

These two were Timmy's parents.

Even in death they had remained near their son. Or so Santa liked to believe.

In reality, they had remained because they knew food was above them, out of reach but still there.

What had it been like for the boy? To peer down through a crack in the trapdoor to see his parents in the hallway; desperately trying to get at him, to hug him one last time before they devoured him alive.

With a weary sigh, Santa raised the machete and pulled the second candy cane he still had, then walked straight at the two zombies. They were pathetic specimens really, all skin and bones. A few slashes of the machete and a stab to the head with the candy cane and the undead couple were down. He kicked the bodies away from where the ladder would come down, then reached up for the pull-string and yanked. The trap door came open, and the folding ladder easily unfolded. There was a loudness when the aluminum frame hit the wood floor, the sound seeming to echo throughout the house. With the machete in his left hand, Santa began to climb the ladder. "Timmy, it's Santa Claus. I got your e-mail. I'm here, son. I'm here to rescue you. You're safe now."

Slowly, carefully, he raised his head over the lip to peer into the attic. It was gloomy but there was illumination, thanks to the hole in the roof.

At first there was no sign of anyone, and Santa felt his heart drop in despair. To come all this way, to overcome so many hardships, only to find an empty attic was too much to bear.

"Timmy?" he said again, his voice all but a whisper.

Then he spotted movement to his right, behind a pile of boxes. It was subtle; barely the shifting of a limb on the dusty floor, but it was movement.

"Timmy?" he said again, and climbed up the remaining ladder rungs until he was standing in the attic. He had to crouch a little, the roof too low for his tall stature. Heel to toe, he crossed the wooded planks, for some reason wanting to make as little noise as possible.

"It's Santa Claus, son. I'm here. You're finally safe."

He cautiously pushed the boxes aside, taking in that the boxes had the words 'Xmas' on them. One box was partially open, and inside he could see tangled Christmas lights and ornaments. One ornament was of a small, four-inch paper plate, the picture of a

Christmas tree made with green glitter and glue. Timmy's name was at the bottom, messily scrawled by a kindergartner.

There was the unmistakable form of what had to be a small boy curled up on the attic floor, huddled as close to where the roof met the floor as was possible.

"Timmy?" Santa said softly. He figured the boy was paralyzed with fright, and no doubt half-starved as well. He was probably out of his mind with terror after his experience.

Santa knelt down near the boy, but about three feet away, as his large girth wouldn't allow him to move in any closer.

"Timmy? It's okay, son. I'm here for you."

He leaned towards the boy, and when he did, the light coming in through the hole in the roof was allowed to illuminate the child slightly more. A sliver of light exposed Timmy's left ankle, the pajamas the boy was wearing pulled up high from when he'd scrunched up. Santa's eyes went right to the ankle, to the small festering wound with the distinct impression of teeth marks.

In the blink of an eye Santa put it all together, what must have happened to the boy.

Timmy, in desperation perhaps, had tried to leave the attic when his parents had wandered away a bit, but no sooner had he descended then they returned to attack him. The boy had struggled to return up the ladder, but had been caught by one leg, maybe even yanked back down. Somehow the child had gotten free, but not before receiving a small bite to his ankle. Maybe one of the zombies had even climbed the ladder, and when Timmy kicked out at it to knock the zombie away, he had been bit for his trouble before he could pull the ladder back up.

A dozen different scenarios came to mind, all with the same terrible result.

The small form stirred, as if waking, and ever-so-slowly, the boy's head began to turn, the rest of the body following.

Santa let out a small gasp as he took in the visage of the boy he'd come to rescue, to save from a fate worse than death—if there was one.

The face, once cherub-looking, was now set in a feral grimace. The lips were bared, the small teeth showing. The eyes were two pinpricks in the gloom, the hands curved into claws.

"Oh no," was all Santa could say.

The boy let out a low hiss, then a guttural growl that was more animalistic than human. He rose as he came out of his hiding place, and stood before Santa, peering up at the large man without fear, the little pale face filled with hunger.

With another low hiss the boy attacked, but Santa stuck out a gloved hand and stopped the boy in his tracks. The child hissed and flailed his arms but could get no closer to Santa. Given the difference in size and weight, it was a simple task to keep the boy at bay. Santa backed up into the center of the attic, where there was more room, always with one hand holding the boy firmly by the head. Timmy moaned and groaned, hissing too, frustrated that his prey was so close yet unattainable.

Santa raised the machete held tightly in his right hand, the metal tip touching the exact center of the roof, right where the two halves met in the center. Even then his arm was only raised halfway, thanks to his height.

He shoved Timmy away from him; not enough to push the boy to his knees, but enough so that Santa had some clearance between them.

"Merry Christmas, Timmy," he said as Timmy hissed and came at him again, mouth open wide, fluids leaking from the corner of his lips.

When the boy was in reach, Santa brought the machete downwards, slicing the small child's head clean off his shoulders. The body fell to the side and through the trap door, to land with a dull thump on the hardwood floor of the hallway. The head rolled away, and Santa went after it. Grabbing it by the hair, he placed it on a small rocking chair, turning the face so that it looked away from him. The mouth still moved, the eyes flicking around.

He raised the machete again, and like the small head was a cantaloupe, sliced it in half, making doubly sure the boy was truly dead.

Standing tall, Santa looked around the small attic once last time, then with another weary sigh and the glint of moisture in his eyes, he climbed down the ladder, the metal creaking the entire time from the heavy load it bore.

Stepping outside, he saw that a few more stragglers had arrived. He dispatched them quickly, though perhaps more violently than he needed to. Instead of just taking them down with the machete, he punched and kicked them, and once on the ground, he stomped their heads into bloody paste.

When he was finished, his chest heaving from the exertion, he turned and strode down the street, his head held high. But to anyone who knew him, if there had been someone like that around, that is, they would have seen a slight lowering of the shoulders, as if the once jolly man was filled with sadness.

Three weeks later.

The twenty or so zombies milling around Central Park in New York all looked up simultaneously at the sound of tires crunching on snow.

Their bodies began to turn, so that the entire group was facing the same way. It was eerie the way they did it together, as if they were all attuned to the same frequency. They didn't move, however, but stayed rooted to the spot, waiting for whatever had made the noise to come to them.

It took two more minutes for something to appear, not that the zombies cared. Things like the concept of time were irrelevant to the dead, only the here and now mattered.

Bushes lined one side of the park, and it was here that a large, all terrain vehicle (ATV) pushed through, crushing the bushes into kindling in a flash.

The vehicle didn't have normal tires, nor only four. The six-wheeled behemoth was more of a war machine, with tires as tall as a man with thick ridges to grab dirt and snow easily; each tire was almost two feet thick.

All four sides were armored, and in spray-paint the words, "Santa's sleigh 2" was scrawled hastily in the preformed metal.

In the driver's seat sat Santa Claus. A cigar was in the side of his mouth and he chewed on it thoughtfully. Across his shoulder was an M60, the oiled metal gleaming in the sun. Santa was a large man, and though the gun was heavy, he was still able to hold the massive weapon. Across his chest was a bandolier filled with grenades, and on each one, written in white with Whiteout, was the single word, Ho, so that all together the grenades spelled, Ho-Ho-Ho-Ho and so on.

The zombies began to shuffle towards the approaching vehicle, and Santa pulled the ATV to a stop, the engine idling loudly thanks to the eight cylinder diesel engine within its bowels.

He'd found the ATV on a military base, and had been pleasantry surprised to find the vehicle in good working order. Hell, it even had a full tank of fuel. Though mostly stripped of armament, after a diligent search, Santa had managed to stir up some more supplies, and more than a few weapons and explosives.

The ATV was now his mobile command base, from where he ranged far and wide searching for survivors worth saving. So far, anyone he'd found had been like the cannibals he'd first come across on his journey, humans barely better than the undead they fought against, nothing but predators, which he would dispatch without mercy.

But Santa wouldn't give up. Somewhere there had to be good people still struggling to survive.

Till then he would do his part to destroy the walking dead, to lower their numbers one at a time until they were all gone.

"Come and get some, bitches!" he yelled, then unslung the M60 and began to fire. Spent shell casings rained down around his feet as a barrage of death was spewed forth.

Bullet after bullet tore into the zombies, not just killing them, but practically pulverizing the bodies, a fine mist floating over the area in a dark red cloud.

Some did a dance of death as they were riddled from head to toe, and finally stopped when a bullet hit their heads, the skulls disintegrating as if they were made of paper mache.

When the last zombie was destroyed, Santa released the trigger on the gun, the cylinder slowing to a stop, smoke coming from each muzzle.

The odor of death and decay filled the air and Santa lit his cigar to mask the smell. He hopped out of the vehicle and stomped heavily in the snow, then began walking amongst the corpses.

They were pretty much nothing but a gory paste, though near the edge of the crowd he found one still moving. Its arms and legs had been blown off, and the body had been riddled with bullets, but the head was still intact and attached to the torso. The eyes rolled up at Santa and the mouth opened in a dull hiss.

Santa shifted the cigar from one side of his mouth to the other, then blew out a smoke ring.

His right foot rose into the air and came down firmly on the twitching head, crushing it into the snow. Brains squirted out around the black boot to splash the snow with rotting meat. Santa scraped the bottom of his boot in the snow, then returned to inspecting the rest of the bodies. When he was satisfied they were all dead, he mounted the ATV and drove off, the diesel engine chugging happily.

Santa moved deeper into the park, planning on leaving it soon to drive into Harlem, before continuing on to Times Square.

He was confident once he hit the streets of New York there would be more zombies to kill than he would know what to do with. Glancing over his shoulder, he took in the large bag filled with LAW rockets, grenades and even a flamethrower.

He was ready for whatever the dead threw at him.

Christmas might have been over but he now had a new mission in life—to kill every damn zombie in the world.

He had nothing else.

Santa drove around a statue with its head missing and slowed the ATV to a stop. Before him was a horde of over eighty zombies with more arriving every second. All were looking at him, and a few at the front had begun walking towards the ATV. Soon, even more were coming from all sides, surrounding the ATV as their hands reached up to grasp Santa.

Santa laughed as he leveled the M60 at the undead mob, and with a free hand yanked a grenade from his bandolier and pulled the pin with his teeth, preparing to throw it into the densest part of the crowd.

Santa took in the pale, dead faces looking up at him from the ground as they completely surrounded the ATV. Within minutes the bodies were packed so thick that even the large ATV would have a hard time pushing free.

He threw the grenade into the crowd, and with his lips cracked into a wide smile as his finger began pressing the trigger on the M60, and with teeth clenched tightly to hold the cigar firmly in his mouth, Santa let out a yell of unmitigated glee. "Okay, assholes, who wants it first?"

ZOMBIES, MONSTERS, CREATURES OF THE NIGHT
OPEN CASKET PRESS
OPEN CASKET PRESS.COM
THE NEW NAME IN HORROR

SUNSET
OF THE DEAD
ANTHONY GIANGREGORIO

CLAN OF THE BIGFOOT
BY ANTHONY GIANGREGORIO
LIVING DEAD PRESS.COM